C000318459

Bedwas Writers' Circle

Telling Tales

A Collection of Short Stories

by members of

Bedwas Writers' Circle

Edited by Barrie Llewelyn

Published by Bedwas Writers' Circle 2010

Bedwas Writers' Circle

Chairperson D. Shelton

Heol Uchaf

Nelson

CF46 6NT

This is a collection of short stories. Characters, incidents, and dialogue are products of each individual author's imagination and must not be interpreted as being real. Any reference to places or people's names alive or dead is purely coincidental.

A CIP catalogue record is available from the British Library

ISBN 978-0-9566483-0-3

Printed in UK by Glamorgan Print, University of Glamorgan, Treforest, CF37 1DL

Acknowledgements

Bedwas Writers' Circle wishes to acknowledge the support of all individuals and organizations who have contributed in the publishing of this anthology.

The Circle is extremely grateful for the financial support received from Llanbradach & Pwllypant Community Council, Penyrheol, Trecenydd, Energlyn Community Council, Caerphilly Town Council and Bedwas, Trethomas & Machen Community Council. In addition we acknowledge the financial support received from Thomas, Carroll (Brokers) Ltd, Caerphilly.

For the front cover of this anthology we have to thank John Varney, one of our Circle Members. Thank you John, we are extremely grateful.

We give a very big thank you to all the staff at Bedwas Centre for their continued support and practical help, which has at times gone far beyond their normal 'call of duty.' As always, their support has been given in a friendly and ready manner.

As the production of this anthology has progressed we have received help and advice from Academi. Academi have always been supportive of Bedwas Writers' Circle and long may this continue.

The Print Unit at the University of Glamorgan has, without hesitation, suggested, guided, recommended options for us to consider in the production of our book. There have been times when members of the Circle have visited the Print Unit and have stood there open mouthed as the print possibilities have been offered to us, by the staff of the Unit. To all of you, the Circle extend their sincere thanks.

It would be neglectful of the Writers' Circle not to give a very special thank you to Barrie Llewelyn who has unstintingly advised, supported and encouraged the vast majority of the 'budding authors.' In particular the task of editing the anthology is one which she 'took on board' without any hesitation. It is probably not an understatement to say that without her help and guidance, the task of producing this anthology would have proved far more difficult. Thank you Barrie.

To everyone else who has supported us, in whatever form, many, many thanks.

Dedicated to our families

Contents

They'll Never Know

Mike Thomas

They'll Never Know

The tree is as he's always known it; squat, ugly, scored with lightning strikes. Its thick trunk twisted and hollow, the bark wrapping it like calloused, ancient skin. Its branches, heavy with leaves despite their age, fan up and out at haphazard angles.

It hunkers, alone, at the edge of the field of rapeseed, as if nothing dare grow near it, roots reaching outwards, probing desperately for company. His legs unsteady, he rests a heavy boot on one that has pierced the earth, wonders for a moment if he'll be able to feel it quiver beneath his sole. If he'll be able to feel *her*, somehow.

Her favourite place. An hour from the road, through bramble and tufted hair grass that flays hands and shins, waist-high fern and march thistle which grab for clothing, along a muddied pathway long-forgotten to all, it seemed, except his wife.

He'd always hated coming here but she had that way about her: difficult to refuse, an oddly intoxicating mixture of forcefulness, good humour and a hint of reproach. Now, he couldn't stay away.

His head swims with the alcohol, the champagne he guzzled before coming here again, the flutes eventually giving way to gulps from the bottle, then another bottle, another… He closes his eyes. Remembers the last time.

Chin up, she said to him. *Don't be such a grump, it's beautiful here.* And she'd whipped the blanket outwards, let it billow to the ground at the base of the tree. Glasses, strawberries and the same champagne had appeared from her shoulder bag. He'd shrugged, flopped beside her, ate the fruit from her hand. They gazed up at the branches for a while and then he'd looked at her and she was smiling. Content. Whatever problems there were in the world, here she was most at home.

'They'll never know how much I loved you,' he says, and opens his eyes. He yanks the last champagne bottle from his rucksack, pops it. 'They'll never know…'

Chin up.

It was three months ago that her voice first dragged him from his fitful sleep. He'd woken, disorientated, forgetting everything that had gone before and reached across to her side of the bed. He found nothing but cold mattress. Yet it seemed like she was back, whispering it in his ear as he slept. He'd lain there a while, staring into the dark, musing how strange dreams can be, how real her voice had sounded. *You're gone now,* he'd rasped into the blackness. *Missing, my love. Missing… missing…* He'd whispered it, over and over, as if doing so would make it more real, more comprehensible, until sleep took him even as he wept.

Some days later he'd been lost in thought at work, drifting while carrying out some pointless chore, when he heard those two words again. *Chin up.* He'd snapped his head around, demanded to know which of his colleagues had spoken, saw bewildered faces surrounding him in the quiet office and knew it was her again. He'd cleared his throat, lowered his head, eyes on the computer terminal yet seeing nothing but his wife's face. Her green eyes shining at him, head thrown back, those plump lips drawn upwards as she laughed. His skin had greyed, turned slick; he'd made a mumbled excuse as he fought to catch his breath and walked out, wide eyes following him as he staggered through the office door.

Things began to crumble. He heard it more frequently. Bathing, trying to forget, to clear the fog, submerged in lukewarm water with a damp flannel over his itching, aching eyes, she'd be in his ear again. Her voice in his head. He'd be shopping but find himself incapable of making a simple decision. On days off he'd go to the cinema alone and while those around him laughed at the comedy playing out on the silver screen he'd be crying and begging her to stop. It was a constant in his life now. She'd be there, at his side. *Chin up. Chin up. Chin up.*

He thought the money would help him cope; salve the painful memory of seeing her fade away in his arms. Such a huge sum upon her death, but instead he felt more alone than ever: solvent, yes, comfortable now, but nobody to share it with. At a loss, he'd started returning to the tree. Once, twice, then five or six times. He'd fight through overgrown grass and thorn bushes, sorrow forcing his heavy legs through the quagmire at the river's edge, just to sink to his knees and beg her to be at peace, to let it rest. But she wouldn't.

He stopped bathing. He stopped shopping. Drank. Drank until being drunk was the norm, until there were mere flashes of clarity in an almost perpetual fug of booze. He became a shut-in, living amongst the shadows of his house, eating takeaways he'd pay for through a crack in the door, not caring as he thrust another damp fifty into the hands of the delivery driver and told him to keep the change. What remained of his cachet at work soon disappeared; within two weeks he was released. *We know it's been a difficult time for you,* they told him, with no clue how difficult things had become. *But she's been gone a year and we can't carry you any more…*

He kneels at the base of the tree, muscles groaning, head swimming, no sleep again last night. Just her voice, unrelenting, those two little words over and over, like her mouth was millimetres away, her fleshy lips caressing his ear, her breath warm on his cheek.

'They'll never know how much I loved you,' he says again. 'And I never knew how much I would miss you, my beautiful wife…' His throat tightens; he begins to cry. He sweeps a clammy hand over the soil, knowing it's ridiculous but still feeling for her anyway because maybe that will make all of this go away. And maybe everything will return to normal.

He glances around. Sees nobody. Light wind across the golden field, the rapeseed rippling. Leaves crackle above him, branches creak.

'I'm sorry,' he says. 'I'm sorry for not telling you how much I loved you. For not confiding in you sooner and letting myself get deeper and deeper… Everything got too much, my darling. You'd suffered so much already, and the pain in your eyes when I told you…'

His chest hitches as he sobs, bent over and pawing at the soil, the earth cold between his fingers, the sun beating at his back. *I'm so sorry, I'm so sorry, I'm so sorry,* he moans and rocks back and forth with his eyes closed and he sees it once more, sees it just like he's always seen it, every night since it happened: he's drunk too much of the champagne again and they're lying on the warm blanket and he's not thinking straight, he's been living with it for months, the gambling debts and menacing telephone calls and the heavies turning up at their door and she was just so *oblivious, so happy* all the time and he's telling her all of it, finally letting it out and she's sitting up now, sitting up with that pain in her eyes, that look of betrayal as he tells her how much he owes and she's screaming at him, crying and slapping him as she wails how he's ruined them and finally he can't take any more and something snaps, his hands flying to her throat and in that instant he saw his way out, the sacrifice they would have to make…

He gulps air. 'I wish I could take it all back, is that what you want to hear? The money means nothing now.'

He grabs the open champagne bottle, wraps his mouth around the neck and drinks. Sucks at it. Hears the *pop* as he pulls it from his lips.

'You loved this place so much, I did okay, right?' He pours golden liquid onto the ground, watches as it froths, disappears.

'This is for you,' he says, and strokes the grass as if it were her hair. 'Enjoy it, my love.'

His wife's voice again.

'No,' he shrieks. 'Just leave me alone! Please. *Please*. I can't take it back. I wish I could but I can't.'

Chin up.

'Is that what you want?' he shouts, standing. The champagne bottle is empty and swings at his side, clasped at the neck between thumb and forefinger. 'Just to grin and bear this? This madness? So be it…' and he jerks his chin upwards, eyes towards the branches they once gazed upon together. 'I'll keep my chin up and keep smiling and maybe then you'll end this… maybe then you'll leave me alone and I'll never have to come back h-'

He freezes. Drops the bottle, feels it knock against his ankle then roll away.

He lifts a hand, a tremor in his fingers, reaches towards the branch hanging over him, over the spot he's come back to so many times since it happened.

His first thought is that it's a bud, some strange black growth that's caught his eye. Or maybe an insect. A dark grey cocoon. The remnants of a pupa, left clinging by its former occupant. Whatever it is, it's something he's not seen here before. On tiptoes, he pulls the branch towards him. Sees the crosshatched metal, the wire snaking from its base, snaking along the branch and disappearing into the bowels of the tree.

Chin up.

'Oh my,' he says, and lets go of the branch.

Movement behind him. He turns.

Sees the figure advance towards him from the tall grass. A man dressed as he is: rugged boots, shorts, rucksack. Welts across his calves from the thistles. The clothes look odd as he's used to seeing the man in a suit.

'Henry,' the man says.

'Detective Inspector,' he replies. He hasn't seen him in months. He glances to the horizon, sees cars lined there now, sees pulsing blue lights, uniforms shifting in the haze, paper-suited men armed with shovels and police tape.

The man smiles softly. 'Thank you, Henry.'

'How did you know she was here?' he says quietly.

'We always suspected,' the man says. 'We just needed...you know.' And he gestures to the microphone hidden amongst the foliage.

He looks at the tiny bud, the wire. Down to the ground, to the soil he toiled over that evening, that evening when everything caved in on itself. He glances back at the policeman.

'At last,' he says, and walks towards him.

He listens for her as he walks. Listens.

And hears nothing.

Journey Down a Mountain

Terry Davies

Journey Down a Mountain

Shopping the other day, I caught sight of a man that, for an instant, I thought was my old school pal Griff Hughes. I was wrong. He had been killed in an incident we had both attended back in the August of 1972, just after his twenty-eighth birthday. It took me a while to get over that, but as time passes your memory goes into self protect mode and you get on with your life, until something brings it back with a jolt.

Griff had been the eldest of six kids and always had a gang of them and their mates in tow. They all seemed to love that blond headed joker who resembled a teddy bear, with the ever-ready smile and blue eyes.

He was always laughing and his laughter was so infectious we all fell about in laughter, without even knowing what we were laughing at. He never married; he didn't't have to because there was always a beautiful creature holding on to his arm and batting her eyelashes at him. It must have been the 'Old Spice' aftershave he used! He had a mania for the outdoors and everything military. Even as a kid, he carried an old tobacco tin, containing striking flints, magnifying glass, fishing line with hooks stuck in a cork and matches. In his other pockets he had a ball of parachute cord and sheath knife. I used to call him 'Sparky', because he was always lighting fires, either to roast chestnuts, or to boil a billycan to make tea or just to sit next to on a winter's day. He had a passion for 'Fisherman's Friends' and 'Victory V' cough sweets and his breath always smelt of them.

Griff and I had started school together back in the 1940s, went right through Grammar School and finally joined the Royal Marines together. He went to the Middle East and I to the Far East. I distinctly remember our company being mustered on the main deck of HMS Cardiff one sultry evening before putting into the port of Hong Kong.

The sun was sinking like a giant orb in the western sky; the decks reverberated to the ship's engines beneath our feet and the air was filled with the plaintive cries of sea birds. The taste of salt was on our lips.

Doctor Billingham was to give us a lecture on the sexually transmitted diseases that could be picked up in the Far East. He was a dour Scot with a thick black moustache and the facial expression of one suffering from a severe stomach upset. He began by puffing furiously on his long stemmed pipe. Still pulling on his pipe, he began by saying, 'When we dock, some of you chaps, no doubt, will be visiting the ladies of the night, puff, puff, and will, no doubt, be putting your private parts, puff, puff, where I wouldn't put the end of me walking stick! Puff, puff. Do you understand me, gentlemen? Any questions? No? Good! Enjoy your stay in Hong Kong.'

Following our stint in the Forces, Griff and I met up again a few years later and joined the Glamorgan Fire Service.

* * *

I had promised to take my grandson, Iuan fishing for a long time, so when his birthday arrived, on the 14th

August 2008, I was duty bound to take him. The boy was eight years old and fishing mad.

'Will you take me to the Horse Pool on the Taff, Daddo?' he pleaded. 'Gethin Rees caught a four pounder there last week and it took him half an hour to pull him in. Can we please, Daddo?'

I groaned inwardly at the very name of that pool, but a promise was a promise and I didn't have the heart to deny him on his birthday, so off we went. As I watched my grandson set up his fishing tackle, I felt a warm pride that only the young can bring. The bait was set, the line cast and the waiting began. On the opposite bank a large chasm of a pipe yawned at us.

The river water was as clear as day, waterweed and plants grew in abundance; fish swam lazily through the fronds of vegetation waving in the undercurrents of the water. The metallic blue of a kingfisher was plainly seen as he preened his feathers in the lower branches of an overhanging tree. The morning was warm and sunny, a slight breeze sighed through the branches of the towering beech trees that grew on the banks of that ancient river. The rustling of the branches overhead and the dappling of sunshine and shadow on the water had an hypnotic effect on the watcher. I thought of Griff, I remembered the summer of 1972.

* * *

'Where does this sewer discharge?' I asked him.

'The Sub told me it exits into the Taff half a mile down the valley and I expect those bloody kids will be out and having their tea before we get that far, but we've got to look for them. They were seen to enter this pipe but no one has seen them come out,' replied Griff.

'Well let's get a move on then; the main tunnel is only about four and a half feet high, far too low to walk through. I don't fancy crawling through this lot. I bet those little buggers could run through here without any problem at all,' I grumbled.

'Now come on now, Davies, don't forget I know you,' he said, prodding me in the ribs with an elbow. 'Who was it we lowered over the Garth Quarry by an old rope to rescue his old dog?'

And so it was we made our way through the ankle deep raw sewage in a crouching crab-like crawl, aided only by the beam of my cap lamp to light our way. Griff had switched off his, keeping it in reserve in case mine became exhausted. As we travelled along the tunnel, trailing out behind us was a guideline that was attached to my breathing apparatus harness. This would enable us to find our way back to the main gallery if the tunnel split.

'Good job it's a fine day, Griff, I wouldn't fancy being down here if it was raining,' I said, and as an afterthought asked, 'Did you catch the weather forecast for today? I wouldn't want any nasty surprises down here.'

'Talking about surprises, look at that bloody rat. It must be the size of my cat,' Griff chuckled, knowing that I could not stand the sight of them. 'They are more afraid of us than we are of them,' he laughed.

"Speak for your bloody self, they give me the heeby jeebies,' was my answer.

'Quiet!' Griff said, gripping my arm. 'I think I can hear voices up ahead.'

Increasing our pace, we very soon came upon two little wide-eyed boys, one of whom was sobbing his heart out, the other unable to speak.

'You're all right now, lads,' reassured Griff, followed by, 'Is it just the two of you boys?'

'Yes, mister,' the boy sobbed.

'Are either of you hurt?' I asked.

'No, mister, only cold.'

Turning to Griff I said, 'You'd better radio back to the boss we've found them and they both appear to be okay.' Turning to the boys I asked, 'What are you crying for now lads? You'll soon be out and back with your mam!'

'Our candle blew out, mister, and when we heard the noise of you breathing through those machines, we thought you were monsters coming to get us.'

Griff tapped me on the shoulder urgently and drew me to one side. Speaking in a low tone so the boys couldn't hear, he said, 'The boss said to get out fast; a feeder dam for the colliery has burst its banks somewhere up on the mountain and the Water Board are unable to tell if the water from it will come our way.'

'Right then, lads, let's go. Let's see if we can get out quicker than we came in.' Each of us taking a child's hand in our own, we moved as fast as we could, back in the direction from which we had come. Then we felt what we had both feared. A cold blast of air whistled passed us. We heard the roar. I shouted, 'Quick! Get the boys close to you, Griff.'

Turning to the two boys I said, 'Whatever happens in the next few minutes you make sure you hold onto old Griff here and don't let go. Now I want you to lie down with your feet pointing down the tunnel. Then take a big deep breath and hold it in for as long as you can.'

The water hit and they were gone, leaving me alone to battle with the taut guideline to which I was still attached. I struggled to free my knife from my pocket against the weight and velocity of water that pinned my arms to my sides. I felt like a fish being played on a line as the water slammed me into the walls of the pipe, first one way and then another. Summoning up the last of my strength, I held the knife in my hand and sawed through the nylon line.

Have to hold on, I thought, as my lungs screamed for air. Then I was whisked away. As I was carried along, I tried to relax with my hands and arms covering my head and face. Must look after what little looks I have, the thought amused me. My cap lamp had been smashed and the facemask had been torn from my face. Thank God, the water doesn't completely fill the pipe, I thought. At least I'm able to breathe.

It felt like an eternity being carried along at an ever-increasing speed until at last, I felt myself sailing through the air, disgorged from the pipe, into the river Taff. Treading the ink black water, I looked around me and saw the two boys on the far bank.

'Where's Griff?' I shouted.

'He's floating under that tree, mister, but he won't answer us when we call to him,' replied one.

When I reached my colleague, he was floating face down and lifeless. The world seemed to have stopped spinning.

'Oh no, not you, Griff,' I turned his face up. His neck was broken. He had died instantly.

'Tommy landed on him when we came out of the tunnel; we heard a crack, then he didn't move any more. Is he dead, mister?'

'Aye he's dead son, my old pal is with His Maker

now, God rest his soul,' I crossed myself as I spoke. Then gently, I dragged his body to the bank and out of the water. Removing my tunic, I covered his head and body, telling the boys as I did so, 'Old Griff wouldn't want the world gawping at him in this state, would he lads?'

The two boys nodded their heads in agreement.

A passing angler volunteered to go for help and very soon fire, police and ambulance personnel were at the scene. The two lads were sent to hospital for a checkup but were released later that day, physically unaffected by their adventure.

I went home alone and spent the rest of the night getting drunk in a futile attempt to hold old memories at bay. Griffith Hughes was buried ten days later, hailed as a hero by the boys' parents and newspapers.

* * *

'Daddo! Daddo! Wake up, Daddo!'

I woke with a start to see Iuan standing in front of me with the biggest trout I had ever seen.

'How in all that's holy did you manage to land that monster? It must be six pounds if it's an ounce.'

'A man helped me and it took all of our strength to play him enough to land him!'

'Man! What man?' I looked around me and saw no one.

'He said he was your friend, Daddo, and he told me to tell you his name was Griff.'

Beaks in the Sloppy Ice Cream

Helen Harris

Beaks in the Sloppy Ice Cream

The sun, like a fiery ball, rose quickly from the watery horizon into the pale blue cloudless sky. A cool on-shore breeze blew across the water creating a ripple effect. The sea's soft relentless sound was suddenly broken by the chugging of a distant engine. A fishing boat was steering a course to the small harbour of St. Ives, its arrival greeted by a welcome party of noisy seagulls which swooped and hovered over the weary craft with delight and anticipation.

Perched on one leg next to a CCTV camera, high on top of the lifeboat station a lone seagull looked down. Turning his head slowly and methodically over his bird's eye view, he was able to observe minute detail. Shifting his weight quickly onto both webbed feet, with a small jump he launched himself off the building and glided effortlessly across the bay towards the pier and landed on the sea wall. Feeling the sun's warmth on his feathers, Sid opened his wings and flapped them a few times.

I've always tried to stay trim, you'd be amazed at how many calories flapping your wings burns off and I try to do thirty flaps and five aerial circuits of the town before lunch. Now that I've reached middle age it's easy to get a bit more spread around the middle so I strive to eat healthily and don't overindulge in left over fish and chips which have unfortunately resulted in the appearance of "batter bellies" on some of my mates.

This has led to problems with their gaits on terra firma and if they are able to get airborne, reliance is placed heavily on eddies, which can prove precarious.

When my ancestors were chicks there were no fast food stalls along the beach and life was very different; survival was dependent on your fishing skills, although it's fair to say the fish population was more abundant then. Last year the colony was becoming increasingly concerned about a growing unruly youth culture. Older chicks would hang around in flocks on rooftops just wanting chips and ice cream, give them a lovely mackerel and they would just turn up their beaks. The parents were warned about chick obesity and the hyperactivity caused by too many "E"s. Numerous campaigns were launched including one by the young gull Jakey, over there. He spent many hours flying around offering advice about healthy eating but it was usually of no avail; some of the parents even took exception and started feeding their chicks junk food. Jakey was nearly ripping his feathers out. Even the tragic event of a young gull choking to death on a greasy chip had little effect.

The behaviour of the younger members of the colony continued to cause concern. They were witnessed: drinking alcohol from cans; firing their droppings onto the sunbathing public and sticking their beaks in the tourists' sloppy ice creams. Ironically, it would be thanks to their unacceptable behaviour that a change of events which would ultimately culminate in the saving of the colony, happened.

It began last summer when the local Tourist Board received a string of complaints from irate holidaymakers. These were levelled specifically at the colony and ranged from raucous behaviour including late night squawking to physical assaults, especially on small children. The Head of Tourism had numerous meetings with local councillors concerned about a possible reduction in revenue to the town. This prompted the council to take action and a statement was issued in which we were categorised as vermin and placed as a top priority. The colony felt we were being unfairly victimised and the council's response was disproportionate to our crimes. Meanwhile the real vermin, the rats, who had consistently remained at the top of the council's list, simply fell off the authority's radar. The rats were cunning and ensured their nocturnal antics were seldom encountered by the tourists and they deliberately kept a low profile on campsites and caravan parks. As a result they had a huge population explosion - a sort of rat boom. Personally, I would have fumigated all the known rat packs as, to us, they are brutal murderers who try to steal our eggs and eat our unborn chicks.

Part of the council's action plan to eradicate us (everyone has to have action plans and mission statements nowadays) was to adorn that ghastly Tate Modern with lethal metal spikes. Initially, several surveys were undertaken to assess each outside ledge which could be construed as a perch and then numerous measurements were taken. This white building became known to the colony as the "white elephant" with nowhere to put a webbed foot. Rumours circulated that there would be a plague of council "spikes" on several other public buildings, as the council attempted to purge the town of its gull population.

Whilst policies were being rubber stamped in the Town Hall, news of our behaviour was reported in the local press. One pompous journalist wrote a scathing article which we read - it happened to have been wrapped around some left over chips. It later transpired that his young daughter had been dive-bombed by a flock of young gulls and her tutti-frutti ice cream with double Flake had been stolen. The colony was furious; this savage criticism of our youngsters was hypocritical when he was feeding his own child junk food. As one vocal gull said in our Extraordinary General Meeting, she should have been chewing on an apple and stealing the ice cream had done her and her teeth a favour but, strangely, no one from the Council mentioned this. To add insult to injury, he then appeared on the local TV news and his article was printed in the national press, including the broad sheets. We then heard that a national channel was coming down to interview him berating us for the daily news programme.

A huge TV crew arrived the following week and spent ages locating their cameras and checking the light; you've never seen such a palaver. They filmed a huge flock of us descending onto the beach; well we knew they were there, word had spread amongst us and, to be frank, we were all vain and wanted to appear on the telly. Arrangements were made to meet out at sea where we gave ourselves a thorough preening. The whole event was organised with military precision and each bird knew exactly what he had to do. Initially we swooped in and circled the town and then we performed a series of spectacular mid air stunts including figures of eight and flights in formation before making a perfect landing on the beach. Some of us unfortunately landed on the cameramen and their equipment - well there were so many of them you could hardly see the sand!

When televised, our aerial display caused a huge sensation amongst ornithologists who had never observed this behaviour from gulls before. Such was the impact of the news report that three days later half the crew from a popular nature programme arrived with more cameras and a garrulous bearded presenter called Will. The colony thought it was a hoot but the council were not so pleased.

The arrival of this production team coincided with that of half the bird watchers in the U.K. and some from abroad, who all sported the biggest collection of binoculars and telephoto lenses I've ever seen. By then we had these aerial displays off to a fine art, varying the content and the times during the day. That kept the "twitchers" on their toes, never knowing when the next display would happen. Actually, it was doing wonders for the colony, we were all much fitter and it was a friendly social event like an avian Ceilidh.

The production team set up spy cameras just about everywhere; it was like Big Brother. They were located on rooftops, in shop windows and even disguised as a boulder on the beach. The latter was so obvious; we hardly get a pebble on the beach let alone a huge plastic boulder. Some of the gulls would clean their beaks on it and give it a good pecking which peppered it with holes and made the camera crew very uneasy. It turned out to be very expensive. In fact, sabotaging their equipment became a fun sport. We built nests in front of cameras, stuck feathers in the wiring and tried to get our bird droppings to land on the "twitchers" and cameramen below.

Unfortunately some members of the colony found the cameras too intrusive and there was a small exodus of gulls from St. Ives wanting to relocate to the country. Fortunately we had two gulls that could assist them in finding their dream nest: Paul and Kristy. He was a pleasant gull, thin and leggy but nice to talk to. Kristy however was another story. She was a big bird with an ego to match and a terrible snob, screeching at you as if she had a pebble stuck in her beak. Coming from a privileged upbringing (her family nest being on the top of a leading fish restaurant in Brighton) gave her little understanding of the struggles of the ordinary working gull.

Over the winter months the local accommodation was fully booked with birdwatchers, photographers and film crews and gull merchandise flew out of the plethora of artists' galleries. Overall everyone was happy; even the council had now reluctantly recognised that we are a valuable asset to St. Ives. They are now running a national competition to design a large gull statue which will dominate the harbour. The colony is having a great time and we view ourselves like the Red Arrows, a professional team who perform spectacular stunts to a grateful awe-inspired crowd.

We never perform our displays at meal times when the news comes on, we like to keep abreast of current affairs. Luckily there is a small television shop with a giant screen in the window. We position ourselves on windowsills nearby and those, whose vision is not too sharp, stand on the pavement outside. Unfortunately there is no sound but we've become adept at lip reading, although we sometimes get information and names muddled up.

We were all riveted to the television during the recent general election, especially the debacle about who would be Prime Minister. All those meetings and behind the shiny black door deals culminating with that appearance of Nick Clagg and David Cameroon in the rose garden, it was better than a soap opera. In the end we all ended up with a BOGOF or VOGOF offer, instead of buying we Voted One Got One Free. An array of presenters came out of the wood-work and as for all those polls: there was even a poll of polls. Opinions were voiced from dull ex-ministers, who you hoped had long departed the corridors of power only to discover to your chagrin that they now wore ermine and occupied seats in the Lords, where only death could stop them. Those MPs really think we are all gullible.

Well, time for me to fly. I need to do some warm-up exercises followed by another circuit as we have two technical displays today.

Sid launched himself into the air and effortlessly hovered for a few seconds. Then finding a suitable eddy he was soon soaring high above the bay. Below him vendors were opening early in an attempt to reverse the credit crunch. Eager "early bird" families were setting up mini versions of their sitting rooms on the sand while their children squealed with delight and waved fishing nets and buckets. A surly group of teenagers stopped digging two large holes, in which they hoped they could bury their controlling parents, to watch an uncoordinated Dalmatian puppy chase some of Sid's cousins across the sand.

Sid was now a distant spot on the azure horizon. This spot moved rhythmically up and down as he practised his solo for the aerial displays later.

Gardeners' World

John Varney

Gardeners' World

It was surprisingly mild for a March afternoon as I set off with my father to the North Notts Allotment Association. The purpose of our journey was to make the yearly purchase of seed potatoes for my Dad's allotment. I pushed the wooden wheelbarrow along Sherwood Street, up Titchfield Hill until we eventually arrived at the Association hut. The last part of the journey was along an unadopted road. The wheel of the barrow crunched on the cinders where the residents had emptied their ashes to give the surface greater stability. The Association hut was absolutely huge and to me it was akin to entering a cathedral. Along the length of the cathedral sat the patriarchs perched on bags of various varieties of seed potatoes. They greeted my Dad with assorted grunts and nods. They were of different heights and weights but the common factor was that they all wore caps and looked very old.

At the far end of the cathedral was the high altar. This was dominated by an enormous pair of metal weighing scales. The balancing arms stretched out on each side like a rusting crucifix. The incense from the patriarchs' pipes floated in the air, mixing with the smell of blood fish and bone fertiliser, damp sacks and potash. It was a cocktail that seemed to thread its way into your very pores and I thought I could smell it on my body for days afterwards. One of the patriarchs aroused my interest more than the others. His name was Percy and he looked as if he'd been made up from an old rag bag. His head looked incredibly large and his face carried an expression of absolute dejection. He appeared as if he'd never experienced any sort of love. His waistcoat was very badly stained and there were no two buttons the same. Several were missing. I watched as his tatty old waistcoat seemed to rise and fall independently of his breathing. I suddenly remembered that I'd always been told it's rude to stare. Nevertheless, I couldn't resist occasionally gawping at the strange movements taking place in the grubby waistcoat. Slowly Percy took his pipe from his mouth; there was a glistening skipping rope of saliva from his chapped lips to the end of his pipe. This rope eventually obeyed the request of gravity, falling on his waistcoat and was gradually absorbed into the material. He took from his pocket what appeared to be a strange penknife and started to clean out the bowl of his pipe, tapping out the residue of his efforts on the side of his boot.

The door suddenly opened and the instant draught caused a string of cobwebs, just above Percy's head, to ripple like the tutus of a corps de ballet. The late arrival was greeted by, "George," which seemed to bounce from one mouth to the next. Percy had now taken a tin of tobacco from his pocket and momentarily, as he opened it, a delicious smell as of some exotic fruit pervaded the hut. Percy kneaded the tobacco between the heels of his hands, as if he were trying to resuscitate some small delicate animal. He then took his strange penknife and packed the bowl of his pipe as if he were priming a musket. Slowly he patted the four pockets of his waistcoat with a negative expression. Without a word being spoken, George threw him a box of matches. Percy struck a match and the smell of phosphorous filled the musty air. He pressed the match box on the top of the bowl and his lips pursed like a contented baby as its mother's breast. He placed the box of matches in one of his waistcoat pockets and George made a tacit *tut tut* and wiped his nose on the sleeve of his greasy boiler suit. I presumed he'd come straight from work.

Someone had inaudibly broken wind. There wasn't a single comment from any of the conclave, but an exceptionally tall man called Sid made a very hasty departure. He looked like Mr. McGregor in my Beatrix Potter book and he walked with a very peculiar gait. The corps de ballet above Percy's head performed a very ragged arabesque as Sid hurriedly slammed the hut door. Just left of these cobwebs was a very yellow, faded, foxed newspaper cutting about planting potato peelings. The drawing pins at the corners of the cutting had rusted, leaving a residue, which had run in the dampness and looked as if the pins had been bleeding. The article was headed 'Waste Not Want Not' and was obviously something to do with the war, but I was far too young to remember that.

Suddenly the patriarchs started to preach their ideologies. Percy was obviously the bishop from the Diocese of 'Pentland Javeline'. His sullen face almost, only almost, broke into a smile. Charlie, a man with a cauliflower ear and the remains of his dinner in the corners of his mouth, brought salutations from the Diocese of 'Arran Pilot'. My Dad, to my amazement, was ordained into the church of 'Sharpes Express'. Perhaps I shouldn't have been surprised, bearing in mind he was a railway man. Walt, who was also the treasurer of the Association, brought greeting from no lesser person than the 'Duke of York' himself. Walt had a strange habit of rubbing the back of his neck and then sniffing his fingers.

I felt completely disorientated in the company of these elderly clerics. I was thoroughly at a loss to know what was significant. I wanted to reach out to these men, if only they would talk about Meccano crane pulleys or that new programme on the wireless, 'Ray's A Laugh'.

Without warning, I was aware of Walt nudging me quite hard in the ribs offering something in a small tin with the name 'Imp' printed on the side. Into my hand fell a minute black cushion.

'Goo on lad,' he said, 'thems not on points.'

I popped the strange tiny piece of coal into my mouth. At first, it tasted vaguely like liquorice, but gradually a horrible, vile taste developed in my mouth and my throat started to burn. I was completely at a loss as to what to do; the roof of my mouth was now well alight. I looked at Walt. Blackish saliva was running from the corner of his mouth, down his chin and dripping onto a list of his requirements. His hand moved towards his jacket pocket as if to offer me another *do it yourself poison kit.* I shook my head furiously and pondered why a square of Cadbury's chocolate didn't last as long as this pungent lozenge. The inside of my cheek had gone numb as if I'd had an injection for dental treatment. I began to understand why Imps didn't need points, but I just couldn't work out how I was going to get rid of the foul bitter jube.

Eventually the patriarchs were blessed with their seeds, which would, in the fullness of time, manifest into a trinity of mash, chip and roast. The men reverently genuflected before the weighing scales, as they swung their sacks of potatoes over their shoulders.

The loveless Percy now rose heavily from the broken chair he'd been occupying and again there were strange movements inside his squalid waistcoat. I thought, *perhaps it's T.B.* I knew that that had something to do with your chest.

As I left the huge hut, I felt I had been present at some ritualistic ceremony, performed by the elders of a primeval tribe. As soon as Walt was out of sight I spat the now piece of black grit onto the cinders and continued to spit into the gutter at about every five steps.

'Don't to that,' my Dad said, 'it's common.' I fell quite a long way behind him and continued to gob. By the time I got home, I was absolutely parched and I ran the tap until the water was icy cold and I drank thirstily.

'Did you see Percy's ferret under his waistcoat?' asked my Dad.

'Oh! Does it love him?'... I dearly hoped so.

How I Hunger for Your Touch

Mary Thomas

How I Hunger for Your Touch

The fateful words 'ashes to ashes, dust to dust' keep reverberating around in my befuddled brain.

I stood apart from the gathered throng of people and I watched them standing nervously, their feet shuffling at the graveside. I watched from behind a large yew tree as they pulled up the collars of their coats and huddled under their black umbrellas as they lowered his coffin into the sad, little hole in the ground. I watched, unseen by the mourners, as they walked away from the churchyard and made their way to their cars parked outside the rusting, wrought iron gates. When no one was about and the gravedigger had filled in the grave and placed the mountain of wreaths around it in a neat pile, I sneaked a little closer. There, oblivious of the rain and the hateful wind cutting into my grief ridden body, I threw myself onto that grave and cried out to the heavens above.

'Don't leave me, Marcus! Take me with you! Please, don't leave me alone.' How long I stayed there shedding tears for the man I loved I cannot recall, all I remember of that dark, dreary day is someone bending over me, and leading me away.

I have no idea where he took me. I knew it was a man, I could smell the pipe smoke on his clothes as he wrapped his arms about me. Neither do I have any idea where I am at this precise moment. I do know that I am not alone, people keep coming into the room and sticking needles into my arm as I lie in this unfamiliar bed, and I know, on the odd occasions I have been awake, there has been a woman, dressed in black, like a female grim reaper standing at the foot of the bed. She's there again now, staring at me with hooded brown eyes. There is a man with her too, middle aged, grey haired and portly, he has half-rimmed glasses perched on the end of a bulbous nose. She sees that I am awake and immediately she pounces.

'What can you tell me of the accident, Mrs. Patterson?'

What accident? Where? When? She has asked that self same question over and over again during the time I have spent in this lonely bed.

She tries another approach, friendlier, using my first name.

'Christine,' she gushes at me. 'You do know that Marcus is dead? There was a terrible accident!' At the very mention of his name, I cry. Sobbing uncontrollably, I nod in answer. Of course, I know he's dead. I'm not mad! Or am I? Is that what these strangers are trying to determine?

The woman, whose eyes show a rather mean streak turns to the man beside her and says, 'This is getting us nowhere, Doctor. I've tried everything, gone down every avenue to no avail. What do you suggest I do next?'

He doesn't reply at first, just gives her a withering stare, showing his contempt at her lack of compassion. He pulls a chair to the bedside and lowers his bulky frame onto it. He reaches across and picks up my limp hand.

'Kitty!' he says softly. I look in his direction and I'm conscious of tears rolling down my cheeks, I make no attempt to wipe them away. I feel bereft, so bereft that life has no meaning for me anymore. I don't care if I cry my life away.

'Kitty!' The man repeats my name and I look at him through my tear-filled eyes. 'Do you know where you are?' I shake my head. I don't care where I am. I could be in hell for all I care. Perhaps I am!

'You are in hospital, Kitty, you have been here for over two weeks, you have been extremely ill. But for the speedy action of the verger you would have died.'

'I wish I was dead,' I sob. 'I wish I could die at this very moment.'

'I don't think you mean that, Kitty. I suspect that you simply cannot come to terms with what has happened. Your grief over the untimely death of your lover must be...' I cut him short by snapping at him like an angry dog.

'He wasn't my lover! Marcus Armstrong and I never slept together. He was too much of a gentleman to do that. I am a married woman and he wouldn't take what didn't belong to him.'

'I apologise, Kitty. I didn't mean...' but I hear no more, I drift away and dream of things I try to forget.

***

It is September, 1969 and I am twenty-four years old. The man I adored is dead, leaving me alone and unloved. Oh, Marcus! How I hunger for your touch!

How I have longed to be loved all my worthless, miserable life. Do you know what it is like to spend each and every day with that burning desire deep in your soul with the need to be loved and knowing that there is no one in the whole wide world who loves you? As a child, I gazed enviously at other kids as their protective mothers wrapped them in their arms and smothered them with love. I hungered for that love. I yearned for it, but it wasn't to be, for I had no mother and I was ugly, you see, not pretty like my elder sister, or beautiful like my cousin, Susan, just two weeks younger than I, who had exquisite blonde curls and eyes the colour of the Pacific Ocean. My dark hair wasn't short and curly, it hung about my shoulders in what grandmother called 'rats' tails'. My eyes weren't fetching and beguiling like Susan's, they were piercing green.

'Cat's eyes!' Grandma would say and curl her lip in a disagreeable fashion. 'Kitty cat, by name; Kitty cat, by nature.'

On a daily basis, I was always compared to Susan. To grandma, Susan was everything a grand-daughter should be whereas I was at the bottom of the pile.

Where-ever we went, Susan was always brought out like the best china. Grandma would hold her hand protectively while I trotted aimlessly behind, with grandma forever scolding me saying. 'Stop dawdling, Kitty!'

I remember several instances when we would be out together, perhaps on a rare Saturday afternoon treat, someone would come up to us and say, 'Why, Mrs. Burton, what a pretty girl your young grand-daughter is growing up to be. You must be very proud of her.' Grandma would preen herself then put her hand onto Susan's shoulder and reply proudly.

'Yes, she certainly is!' Susan, pleased as punch at my humiliation would stick her tongue out at me.

Although I hungered for that recognition and the love that went along with it, I had a greater desire burning in my soul and that was to see Susan get her comeuppance.

At twenty-two, I married after a whirlwind romance. Grandma couldn't get me down the aisle and out of her domain quick enough.

Peter swept me off my feet. We met at a dance and he took me home. The following afternoon he was waiting outside the hospital, where I worked as a secretary, with a bunch of flowers. It was August and by November we were married. On our first date he told me how much he loved me. The words were like a magic spell with bright lights and fairy dust dancing before my eyes. My stomach did a somersault, there was a buzzing in my ears and I felt I was floating on air. Someone actually loved me! Before I knew it I was telling him I loved him too.

We set up home in a damp, dismal flat above the local greengrocer's. By Christmas my marriage was over. He rolled in at three o'clock Christmas morning and told me how much he hated me and that he had only married me for a bet, a joke. He stood there, swaying from side to side in our bedroom ridiculing me, saying his mates had bet him he wouldn't wed a girl who was as ugly as Quasimodo. Before leaving, he told me smugly what he had done with Susan at our wedding reception.

I was stung. I was in the depths of despair and very nearly on the point of ending it all when in the February life suddenly took a turn for the better. By a quirk of fate I met Marcus Armstrong.

Owing to his secretary's serious bout of sickness, I had been called upon that day to accompany the senior surgeon into the operating theatre to take notes.

Unknown to me, a new registrar had joined the team but I was too engrossed in my shorthand to take much notice. It was only after we had de-gowned and unmasked that our eyes locked together, his were the deepest blue pools I had ever seen and I jumped straight into them and drowned instantly. The first words he ever said to me were. 'You are so breathtakingly beautiful.' He then asked me my name. I recall he asked me in a teasing manner. 'And does this little Kitty scratch when she is fondled and lovingly kissed like my mother's cats?'

Soon after that he wrapped me in his arms and showered me with the kisses I'd longed for all my life.

After that, barely a day passed when we didn't see each other. We lunched, we dined by candle light, we drove in his MG Midget into the countryside and we made plans for our future. I have to say that Marcus behaved like a perfect gentleman. Oh, we kissed and cuddled, but never went too far. He couldn't or wouldn't, forget that I was a married woman. He assured me that until I was divorced and came to him of my own free will, he would not lay a finger upon me. But getting a divorce was proving to be difficult for my errant husband had absconded, even his mother had no idea of his whereabouts.

I tried to tell Marcus that as I had been cast off like a row of knitting I felt I was a free woman, but it was no use, he wouldn't budge on his principles. I didn't need to sleep with him, it was enough to feel his hand in mine, to receive the occasional wink across a crowded room or the secret telephone call in the early hours of the morning. We loved each other with a passion that knew no bounds. I became aware at that time how addictive love actually is. It is all consuming twenty four hours of each and every day. It's like a drug, you become addicted to it and any form of withdrawal is a nightmare. Your craving for that love becomes stronger and more powerful.

For the first time in my life I was sure that the love I received from another human being was as secure as the Bank of England. How wrong I was.

Marcus and I were out one evening drowning our sorrows, the search for Peter had come to nothing. I was so upset I wanted to break down and sob into my Martini but Marcus just grinned at me and said, 'Cheer up, it's not the end of the world.'

'But it is to me, Marcus. Perhaps you'll get fed up of waiting for me,' I said wiping away a tear.

Marcus kissed me gently on my cheek and said, 'Kitty, for you I'd wait forever.' I felt a sudden surge of joy to be instantly replaced by that sinking feeling in the pit of my stomach. Susan had walked in and immediately made a beeline towards us. Soon she dominated the conversation and within a week I noticed a change. Marcus was edgy and withdrawn. He complained bitterly about Susan, telling me she was making his life an abject misery as she pursued him relentlessly.

A few weeks later she came to my flat. I had barely opened the door when she barged in pushing me out of the way in that self assured bossy manner she has. She strode purposefully into my small living room and stood there holding out her left hand, wiggling her fingers in the air at me. My eyes were immediately drawn to the impressive diamond solitaire on her third finger.

I felt my breath leave my body. I clutched my chest as I felt a pain stab me in my racing heart.

'Marcus and I are getting married,' she said with a malicious smirk on her painted lips.

'No!' I gasped, feeling the room whirl about me. 'It's not true! He is marrying me as soon as I get my divorce.'

She gave me a contemptuous glower, then with a triumphant sneer on her face she declared. 'Tough luck, sweetie! He's mine!'

At that moment, for the first time in my life I saw red. It was like a mist sweeping over my frightened eyes. I heard someone screaming. It was a strange high pitched wail. It was me. I lunged at her and put my hands around her throat and began to throttle the life out of her as I saw the love I had hungered for all my life disappearing before my eyes. It was at that moment, as the red mist started to fade that I realised, just in time, what I was doing. I ran away, leaving Susan coughing and spluttering and gasping for breath on the hearthrug. I ran until I could barely run any more. I ran until I reached Marcus's house. I hammered on the door and shouted so loudly, it was enough to wake the dead. He was not amused on opening the door to find a demented banshee with wild, burning eyes staring at him across his threshold.

'Why Marcus, why?' I stormed at him.

'Why what?' he asked, calmly scratching his head at he did so. I could see by that movement that he was at a loss to understand what I was saying.

'Your engagement to Susan. She's been to my flat and shown me the ring.'

His beautiful eyes opened wide with shock and I heard him take a sharp intake of breath.

'I don't know what you are talking about, Kitty! She's playing games with you. I've already told you that she is making my life an absolute misery. She must have bought the ring herself. It's you I love, Kitty.

Body and soul.' He held out his arms and I fell into them.

A week later, I took the Wednesday off work. I had something to celebrate and I wanted to share it with Marcus. Peter had been in contact, he had been abroad, he had met someone and wanted a divorce as quickly as possible. My joy knew no bounds. Marcus and I could now make plans for our future together. I bought a bottle of champagne, some steak fillets and strawberries, for I had decided to sneak into Marcus's house and cook a meal in readiness for his return home from work that evening. I was dancing on air as I skipped joyfully up the pathway to his front door. I slid the key effortlessly into the lock and opened the door. There wasn't a sound in the house as I tripped excitedly down the thickly carpeted hallway and into the kitchen at the back of the house. It was while I was switching on the gas cooker that I heard what I thought was a woman's giggle coming from upstairs. I slipped off my shoes and crept up the staircase. As I reached three quarters of the way up I could see straight into Marcus's bedroom. Empty champagne bottles littered the floor. On the bed were two people with just a thin sheet covering their sweat drenched, naked bodies. I saw Marcus lean towards Susan, I saw him wrap his arms around her and kiss her passionately, and then I heard her say,

'Steady on, Mr. Armstrong.'

'Now look here, Mrs. Armstrong,' Marcus responded playfully.

On hearing those fateful words, 'Mrs. Armstrong' the red mist once again drifted across my eyes and with burning tears almost blinding me I dashed down the stairs and ran into the kitchen. I grabbed at my shoes and tucked them under my arm then I purposefully turned up the gas jets on the cooker. I opened the back door and rushed through it leaving it open to the elements for a high wind had blown up giving more draught. It wasn't long before the curtains that hung at the open kitchen window began to smoulder.

With tears of grief blinding my eyes I flew down the long narrow garden and stood under the mighty willow and watched as the smouldering flame became a raging inferno. I felt no remorse for what I had done. They didn't stand a chance, for they were so drunk from sipping too much champagne and so wrapped up in their love that they were oblivious of their surroundings.

As I stood there, watching the flames lick through the building I asked myself, 'What have I ever done to be so unloved?'

What hurt me most was the fact that not even Marcus loved me. He, who told me each and every day how beautiful I was and how much he loved me, lied glib words I realised too late. Words that are so easy to say, but so hard to mean. Oh, Marcus! How could you? I would have forgiven you anything had it been anyone else but Susan. She, who had stolen my grandmother's love, had finally stolen the love of the man I adored with every fibre of my being.

May God forgive you, Marcus, for what you have done.

Will I ever be able to forgive you? No! Never!!!

The Spell

Helen Murphy

The Spell

Look! Look at him! There he stands: tall, gaunt, austere, rod in one hand, whilst with the other he draws marks on the wall - indecipherable to ordinary men. A book is open on the table - a table on which there is a cover showing lovers embracing. As we used to do.

It has been many years since we were young. He was handsome then. The hair, now grey and covered by a skull cap, then flowed down onto his shoulders in ringlets. His eyes were dark brown and as soft as the velvet covering the antlers of a kid. Once, they laughed with glee and looked at me with adoration; now they look, but do not see what he has become: obsessed.

Look! In the inglenook there sits a man, his friend, his co-worker, the cause of his demise as the man I knew. They are both staring at a skull. It is the cause of their madness.

When we were young, he and I, we would meet in a room hung with sumptuous tapestries; he would sing words of romance to me, stroke my hair and swear his undying love. Sometimes we would ride behind the baying hounds, the wind rushing past us, the horses' hooves pounding, pounding. It was good to be alive. Afterwards, we would kiss and express our passion in moments of sweet surrender.

When I became with child we thought our joy was complete. But it was the beginning of the end. One night, as he chased me in a lovers' game, I tripped and fell. Our baby died and, soon afterwards, so did I.

He was distraught. He felt he had no reason to live. He had lost his love and there was no future for him, he thought. For months he locked himself in his room. Then he began to read books, books of a certain sensibility, of a subject matter that is against the law - of the church, of the rules of life itself!

He emerged, utterly different from the man I had loved. His eyes were wild and he had the look of the maniac. Careless with his dress, of what he ate, he had no desire for contact with those he had known all his days and who loved him dearly. He consulted with many scientists, seeking the answer to the question which possessed him - can the dead be brought back to life? Our Lord and Saviour, Jesus Christ, has taught us that this is so - but in His time, not ours, and in His way, not ours.

At last he met the man in the corner. Rodolpho is his name. Together they pondered until, in the depth of night, they visited a graveyard.

They brought bodies back to this bare cell where they did unmentionable things, all in an effort to prove that they have the power of life and death. They failed. But they are driven... still. He dresses in black, like a teacher or a cleric, but it is the black arts he studies, not the ones that prepare children for a hopeful future or bring succour to a grieving heart.

He believes that one day he will hold me in his arms again, that we will love as we used to do. I love him. I have always loved him. I have never left his side. My skull lies there as he speaks his incantations but I will ne'er return to him, for I am spirit, not flesh, and spirit I will remain.

Inspired by the painting "The Spell" painted in 1864 by Sir Fettes Douglas displayed in the Scottish National Gallery, Edinburgh.

Hot Spots

Gareth Scourfield

Hot Spots

'Emergency. Which service do you require?'

'It's Colin, my husband. He's got a problem.'

'Is your husband ill?'

'Well, yes and no really. He says he's on fire.'

'ON FIRE!! Good grief, madam, it's the fire service you need!'

'Oh, I'm not sure if I need the fire service. He's not in flames or anything, but he's screaming in agony. He says that his backside is burning.'

'So, do you want the Fire Service or not?'

'I'm not sure now. If they came along, what could they do for ... Hang on, hang on a minute please. What's that, Col? Don't be so stupid. Of course they aren't going to come here and hose you down. Now just lie there for a minute whilst I speak to this nice man on the telephone. Sorry about that, love, he was a little bit agitated then. What were you saying?'

'If he's not on fire but still has a problem, then I think you'd better speak to someone from the Ambulance Service. I'll put you through straight away.'

'Col, they are putting me through to the Ambulance people. Are you alright? I haven't heard you groan for a minute or two. You are not unconscious are you? Oh that's better; I can hear you groaning again now. Look, love, I know you are in pain, but please try your best not to roll around on that new carpet. I don't want it marked or stained or anything!

Well that's not a nice thing to say and anyway there's no need to swear at me like that. Don't forget, that carpet hasn't been fully paid for yet. You stain it and you'll be out, mind. You can go and live with your bloody pigeons for all I care.'

'Ambulance Service, can I help you?'

'Oh hello, love. It's my husband, although I'm starting to wonder for how much longer he'll remain my husband, mind.'

'Is he ill?'

'Well he says he's dying, although I'm not too sure myself. Oh hang on, hang on a minute please: COLIN, get your backside off that settee now! Don't think I can't see you! Sorry, love, you were saying?'

'Are you saying he's ill, but that in your opinion, he's not dying? Is that correct?'

'Yes, that's about it. Oh I'm so glad I got through to you. You sound as if you've got a good head on your shoulders you have. Do you live local because you don't half sound like our Jack's daughter? She's a nice girl she is. You are not her are you?'

'No I'm not her, but thank you for asking. Now then, I really do need to determine what the problem is with your husband.'

'Silly bugger, that's what he is. He won't admit that he needs new glasses, that's his problem.'

'Look, madam, this is the Ambulance Service, not Specsavers. If you are ringing to ask us to do an eye test, then you are going to be unlucky. We deal with emergencies. Now let's get back to basics. What exactly is the problem?'

'Well he's rolling around on the floor, screaming in agony, that's what the problem is.'

'If he's screaming, can we assume that he's not got a breathing problem?'

'Breathing problems? As God's my witness, he'll have a real breathing problem if he tries to get up on that settee again. I'll throttle him I will.'

'Madam! If you don't tell me what's wrong, then I'm going to pass on your threats to the police. It's up to you!'

'Yeah, sorry about that, love, but you need the patience of a saint to live with him. Are you married? Because if you are then I hope you haven't got one like mine. He keeps pigeons, but he would be better off keeping pigs. I think he'd be more at home with pigs. Probably relate to them better. Hang on again, love… yes, that's right, Colin, it's YOU I'm talking about. DON'T YOU SWEAR AT ME!! Don't forget, I'm your only link with the outside world and if you keep on like you are, you'll soon be outside this world, if you get my gist.'

'MADAM for the final time, will you please tell me what the problem is with your husband?'

'Tried to do it in the dark, didn't he. Too bloody tight to put the electric light on, wasn't he.'

'What exactly did he try to do, Madam?'

'Put his ointment on himself, didn't he.'

'And what ointment was that?'

'His pile cream. Oh he's a martyr to his piles he is.'

'And something went wrong?'

'If I've told him once I've told him a thousand times, don't leave your ointment just lying around. He just uses it and then leaves it anywhere. Next time he needs it, it's always a case of 'Have you seen my cream, love? I know it's here somewhere.' Well I had him.

Last time he left it lying around, I put it away in the drawer along with all the other creams and ointments we've got.'

'And has be applied something in error?'

'You got it in one, love.'

'Do you know what he used?'

'Course I do. He used Ralgex didn't he! Oh you should have seen him jumping about. Pity there isn't an Olympic event for synchronised jumping and screaming, because I reckon he'd be in with a chance of a medal. Trouble is, when he put the Ralgex on, he went over a bigger area than he needed to. All over his bits, if you know what I mean. You do know what I mean, don't you?'

'Yes, Madam, I know exactly what you mean. It must be very painful for him. When did he apply it?'

'Oh it must have been about eleven o'clock last night. He must have screamed in agony until gone midnight, but then, luckily, I managed to drop off to sleep. I think the pain must have eased for him at some point, but there again, I suppose sleeping in a bath of cold water must have helped him. I wouldn't have bothered dialling 999 this morning, but when I saw his bits, well they were like two big blood orange look-alikes. Oh I felt so sorry for him. That's when I thought that I'd better get help.

First off I phoned a young girl living just a couple of doors from us. She's in the St John's Ambulance, she is. I asked her if she could pop around and tell me what I should do. To be honest, she wasn't much help, mind. All she did was giggle, take some photos on her phone and said she'd show all her mates. Col swore a lot at that point and I thought it best if she left.

I then went up to Dan Jenkins's, the Chemist, for

advice, but apart from telling me to speak to my GP, he couldn't really offer anything else. Mind you, I've got to be fair, it was handy for me going there, because whilst in the village I managed to get our pensions and then I had a coffee and a quick chat in the café with my sister, before getting the next bus back. So you can see, this is the first chance I've had to ring 999.'

'I think under the circumstances, Madam, my advice to you is to take your husband to your GP, or if that's a problem then go straight to your nearest A&E Department.'

'If I don't, what could happen to him?'

'Well, I'm not too sure, but I suppose there's always a chance that if the pain persists, he could go into shock and then suffer further problems. One thing I do recommend, is that he continues to take cold baths and that if you have any soothing cold cream, then you apply it to the affected areas for him. Is that alright?'

'Oh I'm not sure about rubbing cream all over him. What if he comes over all unnecessary? Oh I don't want that at our age and him with a bum looking like the Japanese flag. No, no, it's going to have to be one of the other options.

I don't think he'll go to the hospital, because it's either two buses or a taxi. Well I can tell you now, he won't pay what the taxis charge and I don't think he'll want to go on the bus. He's already told me that he doesn't think he could suffer wearing pants and trousers at the moment, and he certainly wouldn't go on the bus without them. And as for the Doctor's, I don't think he'll fancy sitting in that waiting room wearing my old dressing gown. He hasn't got one of his own, says real men don't wear them, and if I'm honest, I don't think a delicate shade of cerise is his colour.

Tell you what love, I'll have a think about it and I can always ring you back. Thanks for your help.'

Phone goes down.

'Colin, love, I've got some bad news for you. The ambulance woman doesn't think there's much they can do for you. Her only suggestion was that I should get in some white bread and a couple of tins of ham, just in case like. Oh, and one other thing, she also suggested that you try to get the best price for your pigeons. Now if you don't mind I'd like to watch the telly for an hour or so. You lie there quietly now, but don't forget, you've only got to call me if you want anything, mind.'

The Blind Man

Dinnella Shelton

The Blind Man

At last he returned the drill to the tool box. Pat couldn't get out of the bungalow quickly enough but he needed to say all the right things before he pocketed their cheque.

'Yep, I think you've made the perfect choice, although I had my doubts when I saw them in the showroom this morning. Are you sure you don't want me to put the cleaner over? Let me know if there's any problem.'

He was twitchy again; his eyes felt gritty and his body kept shuddering. He knew they couldn't wait for him to go and the feeling was mutual. What did they know about what was going on in his life anyway? There they were, retired and comfortable changing their bloody furnishings whenever they wanted. Pat slammed the door of the firm's van. No doubt they had a new Audi in the garage. Thank Christ this was his last call of the day. Thank Christ Mazy wasn't going to be there when he got home.

As soon as the fitter left Sarah readjusted the new blinds so the sunlight fell just where she wanted. It highlighted the much prized pastoral scene above the mantelpiece. How she loved to watch her visitors' gaze move to the watercolour.

'Yes, that's perfect but what an odd-ball he was and so fat. Did you see how tight his trousers were? He could barely move in them. I'll just pop the casserole in the oven, John; you pick a red from the rack.'

Pat squeezed the van between two parked cars narrowly missing the tail light of one of them and then he heaved the tool box out. The buggers would steal their granny's toothpick if it could be swapped for dope. He made his way from the front door to the back and headed up the steep garden to the shed. Puffing heavily, he began to lighten-up as he heard the familiar chirping sounds. He jammed the toolbox into the space under the shelf, unbuttoning his trousers as he straightened up. Carefully he removed each of the water troughs from the cages.

'Who's Pat's special friend? Binky, Bullseye have you had a nice day?' The pair of blue budgerigars tilted their heads. 'Gem, Ruby, how are my precious girls?' He puckered his lips and made affectionate sounds. He topped up the seed trays and returned the replenished troughs without spilling any water. After more adoration Pat headed back to the kitchen, put the kettle on and struggled up the stairs to change into his tracksuit. These bloody trousers were killing him. He heard the key in the door before he heard the voice…

'Pat, what the bloody hell are you doing home? Don't tell me you've got no sales again. I've had a gut full of managing on your basic. Get off your fat arse and do some bloody work. I want a new carpet for the living room, and the washing machine's playing up and you burnt the big saucepan when you tried to make chilli last week.' Her voice was as shrill as next door's parrot. 'Get down here will you, give us a cup of tea, I've had a swine of a day.'

He could see by the set of her mouth and the angry way she opened the junk mail that Mazy was in one of her moods. Where was the soft spoken, smiling girl he'd asked to marry him? He handed her a mug and reached for the local free press newspaper which had been squeezed through the letter box.

'Don't get settled into that, we've got things to do. You can start by bringing the bins around the side before those kids take them walkabout. You need the exercise you're like a wallowing bloody whale. You'll need a bed of your own soon if they make 'em big enough.'

As he went out he made an almighty two fingered gesture to nowhere.

'I saw that, you fat pig, just shift yourself.'

He'd tried but he just couldn't. The sweat poured off him as he pulled away and his belly squelched as they disentangled. Mazy turned away and squawked,

'Let's not bother trying anymore; it's not worth the bloody effort. Go and wash, you smell like a river.'

The following morning Pat went as usual to the showroom. His diary told him he had three fittings to do in the morning and two estimates in the afternoon. The estimates were up the Valleys so if he played his cards right he could be finished by four. He didn't hang about for any banter. It seems all the boys could talk about was last weekend's International. So, we'd lost again, so what? To listen to them they should be coaching the side and playing in it.

'Hey, Pat, you'd make a better job in the front row than Jenkins. How about coming training tonight?'

'Piss off, Parry. You're not so bloody speedy yourself.'

'I'll tell you something, Pat. You need to sort yourself out or you won't get through the front door.'

Pat called in Tesco's. He picked up a couple of packs of bacon sandwiches, some drinks and a bag of marshmallows. His first call was on a new estate and he arrived on time. Awkwardly, he manoeuvred the tool box and the roller-blind up the short drive. This one had to be fitted in the upstairs bathroom.

What a bloody squeeze! The window was behind the toilet and the gap between the wash hand basin and the cistern was tiny. Christ, he was struggling. Breathless he stretched to clip the blind into the fitting. Shit! He felt the button go on his trousers.

Back in the van he scrabbled around in the side pocket to see if he had anything he could hold his trousers together with. Nothing. He swallowed a couple of marshmallows and pulled away. Perhaps he would pass somewhere he could buy a belt or even braces otherwise he would just have to manage until he got home.

It was gone twelve o'clock by the time he'd fitted the Venetians in the bay of the modernised terraced house. The owner was emphatic she had asked for the cord pulls to be on the right hand side.

'I will be getting in touch with head office and complaining. I'm not paying you.'

It was only after Pat threatened to take the blinds down that she'd coughed up. No doubt the cheque would bounce.

He was exhausted. What with Mazy last night and the first two calls being difficult he was really behind. He rang the last client of the morning to say he was running late.

'Sorry it's just not good enough, you said twelve noon. You will have to make it after 2.00 now.' The phone call ended abruptly.

Pat drove on. He knew a spot on top of the mountain where he could have his sandwiches and catch an hour's kip. Maybe it wasn't such a bad thing after all. Pat forgot all about the belt he needed.

He pulled up outside 12 Dunraven Terrace bang on two o'clock and saw somebody moving away from the window. Good, the old blinds had been taken down.

Apologising again, Pat got on with fixing the rail. He hoped that she would leave him alone to hang the verticals. His zip kept opening every time he stretched. It was such a bloody fiddly job, clipping on each individual strip. Eventually he stood back to admire the result.

'Mrs. James, the blind is fitted.'

Mrs. James wasted no time in coming into the smart lounge. She screamed loudly and her hands flew to her mouth.

'Get out man, get out, what are you playing at?' He followed her look downwards. His zip had opened again.

'I'm phoning your boss now. I want you out. Out! Out! Do you hear me?'

There was nothing he could say to appease her.

Pat switched off his mobile. There was no way he was going to take another ear bashing today. He'd had a verbal warning after the complaint last month. This could well be the last straw. He wasn't sure it was worth making the afternoon calls.

He called into the paper shop on the way home; his bird magazine would be in. He needed to plan what he was going to say to Mazy. He felt himself beginning to twitch again as agitation took hold. He wanted to talk to Ruby and Gem. They were the only females he could communicate with nowadays. He pulled into a lay-by and skimmed the pages until it was time to go home.

As he opened the front door he heard the familiar music that told him '*Doctors*' was finished.

'Pat, that can't be you, surely?'

There Mazy sat in her dressing gown; the familiar gunge covering her upper lip and chin. Her hair was wrapped in a towel and dark smears dribbled down her brow. And she complained about how he looked!

'Well, what's the bloody excuse today?'

'Give it a rest, Mazy; I'm going up the shed to feed the birds.'

'If you don't bring some more money home they won't need feeding because I'll wring their bloody necks. And you can give up buying those magazines for a start…'

'Hi Binky. I hope you and Bullseye have had a better day than me.' Two blue heads jerked in response. As he poured the seed into their feeders Pat realised he'd left the toolbox in the van. He would get it later; Gem and Ruby were more important. He'd still not worked out what he was going to tell Mazy if things turned out for the worse.

'Pat, get down here quick! Your boss is on the phone he says he can't get you on your mobile. What you been up to now? He don't sound too happy.'

'Shit, Mazy, why didn't you tell him I wasn't home yet?'

Pat was breathless from running down the garden

and he felt a sharp pain in his chest. He listened to the familiar voice.

'My office, 8.30 sharp... And Pat, bring the tool box with you and the spare set of van keys.' The phone went dead.

Pat could hear his heart banging inside his head. Sweat broke out into rivers down his face and that pain came again.

'I'll be there,' he said to no one.

Pat lay awake listening to her snorts. He had no idea where he was going from here. It was while he was trying to think of what he would say in his defence tomorrow that he remembered he'd left his tool box in the van. He dragged himself out of bed and pulled on his tracksuit bottoms. She was dead to the world but still he crept down the stairs. He'd forgotten to put his slippers on and it was icy and wet on the pavement. He scraped his feet on the harsh coconut mat. Thank Christ those kids hadn't been up to their thieving tricks again. He put the tool box down at the foot of the stairs and went to the kitchen. He rummaged in the cupboards and grabbed two Kit Kats. He just couldn't see any way out of this but one thing was for sure she was not going to lay a finger on his precious birds. Wring their necks, would she?

Before Pat went back to bed he checked his tool box. He didn't want 'Super Blind' getting any of his gear. He lifted out the hammer and the spirit level. These were his and he took them covetously upstairs. In bed he nursed the hammer close to his chest. Every snore grinded and pierced his anxious mind. He felt his body shudder again. The pain was returning to his chest and behind his eyes. He gripped the hammer tighter. There was no way out but Pat knew he must protect Ruby and Gem. These little treasures were all that mattered now.

As another pain hit him he heaved himself up and looked down on her, maybe for the last time. Anything can happen to a man in a blind rage.

An Anxious Problem Solved

Julienne Pettit

An Anxious Problem Solved

We are awakened each morning by a chorus of so many birds, cawing, squawking and twittering, a bubbling rise of excitement of life, affirming joyfulness.

This noise comes from a feeding tray which my husband, Colin, has made and attached to his work-shed at the bottom of our garden. Bird food is placed there, and to another bird feeder, three times a day.

As soon as it's eaten up the trays are replenished. The many birds who live in the woodlands opposite our garden, venture across the busy Newport Road to their nearest 'café'! In fact I often remark to Colin that word has got round about this café as we also get a flock of starlings flying over our rooftop. They must come from the small woods nearer the front of the house.

The arrival of the rooks, all dressed in jet-black, recognized as being the biggest of the birds visiting the café, is interesting. Grandfather rook takes centre stage, first in the pecking order. He's bare-faced, dominant and in control. We see this performance many days. Mouths are so full that much drops out, but that doesn't deter them and they refill before flying back to their nests.

The crows come in droves. They seem to be the ones 'on the beat' and they stay together. They, too, have sombre black uniforms, with bright yellow beaks - a symbol of authority. They are quite perky and are allowed to feed with their cousins, the rooks. The crows are well aware of the black and white magpies, with their striking plumage, who have been observing them from a tree overhanging the shed.

When the rooks and crows leave, the magpies decide to take flight and raid the bird tray. They look like coloured Spitfire planes as they dive down. Their piercing chattering sounds, like repeated gunfire, frighten and scatter the birds that have landed on the shed. These aggressive and arrogant magpies attack any defiant birds that remain until they reluctantly abandon the food to return when the attackers have eaten their fill and left.

It really is fascinating to watch the antics of these birds. One who waits, watches and observes until all others have left, is the solitary jay, who flies from the woods to the feed tray, snatches some food and as quick as lightning flies back to the woodlands. We wish it would stay longer because we only get a glimpse of the coloured markings of this beautiful, unsociable and elusive bird, which is known to prefer solitude.

It is also intriguing to watch the flight of starlings as they swerve in a crescent formation, so close together. They arrive when it appears the shed roof is empty, though they do mix easily with other small birds. They like to come to feed, but because there are so many it amazes us that they don't collide with each other. I have tried to count them as they land but it is impossible. They are very noticeable with their black/brown iridescent plumage and have short tails and long beaks and I hear them pecking into the wood of the shed roof.

Often I have heard a bump on the back window and wondered what had been the cause. When I investigate and find the starlings have made it over the roof of our house I am happy. Unexpectedly, three weeks ago, I found a young starling that must have bumped against the wall and knocked itself out. It was squeaking pitifully, it was so distressing. I called Colin, who had looked after many injured birds in the past. He picked it up and tried to comfort it. He could see its wing was damaged and it couldn't stand because one of it's legs was injured. Something had to be done.

While Colin held it, I found a big cardboard box, covered the bottom with some cloth, and then gently added a little food and water before placing the bird inside. We transferred the box to the quiet conservatory hoping that the bird would recover. We carefully observed its recovery for the next two days, by which time it could stand on its injured leg but still couldn't use its wing.

Because the conservatory was getting so hot, Colin suggested we put it in the work-shed. After clearing out many items that could be restrictive, and trying to comfort the injured and frightened little bird, it was then placed in the shed. It was still very frightened and kept hiding itself under an old wardrobe, but luckily continued eating the special food we prepared for him and drinking the water. It appeared to be getting stronger but still couldn't fly, although he tried hard to flap his damaged wing.

Colin doesn't give up on anything that's challenging and this challenge was important to him, trying to help something so helpless. He fixed some wooden strips, about eight inches off the ground, across the width of the shed to encourage 'Squeaky', as we had called him, to flutter up to them. Gradually, each day, he fixed slightly higher perches and eventually

Squeaky reached the highest one, a good thirty inches above the floor. The shed door was left open every day while we sat observing his progress. We were so happy to see him run to the front, then to the back, then flying up to the top perch. After a week of this, a flock of starlings arrived. Squeaky heard them and appeared in the doorway, took courage, spread his wings and joined his natural friends.

To our delight, an anxious problem was happily solved.

Each day the starlings arrive and one sits on the edge of the feeding tray. We hope that it is Squeaky saying 'Hello' to us.

Revenge is Best Served Cold

Gwenda Smith

Revenge is Best Served Cold

'Just give me a minute will you?' I said. Tom had been a right pig since he came home from work. Someone had scratched his car in the car park and you'd think it was me the way he carried on.

I went looking for the Insurance Policy. I thought it must be in the 'CAR' file with all the other documents. While searching, however, I found something much more interesting than a policy, something which I found so interesting that I slipped it into my pocket to read thoroughly later.

At last I found the policy and handed it to Tom to deal with. We had dinner, with little conversation, as was usual in those days. Lately it seemed we had very little to talk about and that night I was more than a little annoyed with him. There was no need to take everything out on me.

Tom disappeared into his study after dinner and I finished clearing up the kitchen before I made myself comfortable on the sofa to read my 'find'.

The envelope was addressed to Mr. T.J. Toynson and looked very official. That's odd I thought, it was obviously important enough to hide from me, but why? I opened the letter which was typed on good quality, headed paper and was from a firm of solicitors in London. It was dated six months ago and I quickly scanned the contents which blew me away. It appeared that Tom had been left a legacy, quite a substantial one at that, from some distant relative I'd never heard of.

Questions were galloping around my head. Who was this mysterious benefactor? Why was the letter in that file? Why had Tom kept it a secret from me? I didn't know what to do next. It was plain that Tom wanted to keep it secret and I was equally determined to get to the bottom of it. I decided I, too, would keep it secret for the time being. I had to have time to think.

I didn't sleep much that night and in the morning I fussed about the kitchen until, at last, Tom left for work. I went straight to the cabinet where all the files were stored and went through each one hoping to find more secrets. I had no luck until I came to 'BANKING'. Now, to give Tom some credit, he dealt with the financial side of everything. He gave me an allowance each month, so although I had no job, I had never needed to worry about money. I'd had no reason to look at his bank statements and obviously he felt that this was a safe place to hide something he didn't want me to find. I never thought he was so comfortably off. We hadn't had a good holiday for years.

What I discovered were a lot more letters from the solicitors. The letter in my hand was the first of many. Now I had the full saga of his new found wealth. He had kept copies of his replies so I had plenty to read. It appeared that the solicitor was one who followed up cases of people who died intestate without any known next of kin. Tom had been traced through census lists and other methods, and was found to be a distant cousin of a reclusive man who had died some time ago. He was the sole heir to a sizeable fortune.

This was only half the story. Inside the file I found a large envelope containing a photograph of Tom with a woman, quite an attractive blonde in fact. On the back Tom had written 'Liz and I at the office party'.

Office party, indeed. I had never been invited to one and now I knew why. I shook out the rest of the contents to find a number of receipts and guarantees - a watch, a bracelet, a diamond ring, even a cashmere coat. My mouth was open. I had never been the lucky recipient of any of these.

I took out his last bank statement. A hotel in York last month, a double room. That was the time he told me he was in a conference in Halifax, very boring it was, or at least that's what he told me. Another hotel in Bournemouth when he told me he was in Birmingham on business. Dirty business I can see now.

This called for some deep thought. I decided not to face Tom for a little while, I had work to do. First of all I logged on to his computer. I knew Tom's password. It was the name of our house so it was easy to find his e-mails. Liz had been in contact nearly every night. No wonder he disappeared into his study after dinner every night. Obviously having him all day wasn't enough for her.

I thought she might like one from me. I didn't sign it of course, simply said, 'Don't you think Tom is fabulous, I think you'll have to move over soon. He fancies me.'

The next few days were as boring as ever except that I e-mailed Liz every day with a new message. Eventually I could see Tom was getting twitchy. I was reading his e-mails from Liz which were beginning to question him on where he was going and what he was doing. As she was whingeing I was getting nicer every day, asking him about his work, suggesting we go on holiday, taking trouble to look good, becoming the perfect wife in fact. I was determined not to dig my own grave by walking out on him, not until I had a share of his good fortune anyway.

So it continued. My financial needs became stronger. I wanted new clothes and good clothes were expensive. We needed things for the house, new carpets, new curtains, all of which cost a lot less than I told him. I said I didn't like driving into town and needed to take taxis. All the extra money went into a new bank account I had opened. I put out feelers for a joint account which would be so much easier for me so I wouldn't have to ask him for money each time I went to town.

It took some time but at least Liz's e-mails had dried up. I still sent her the occasional message asking her advice about weekends away or what to buy him for his birthday, since she knew his tastes better than I did.

This meant that I had Tom to myself. Not that I wanted him, mind you, only his money. At last Tom agreed to have a joint account. I wasn't greedy to begin with, just small amounts which went into my new account but these small amounts became more frequent and if Tom asked I always had a new coat or bag I could show him.

The balance in my personal account was quite healthy when I played my trump card. I remembered a film I had seen once, called 'Shirley Valentine' where the heroine left her home and husband and went to Greece to make a new life. I didn't fancy Greece but had always liked Cornwall. Flicking through the internet I found a house for sale in St. Ives which looked just right for me. It was all I wanted.

On the day I left Tom, I took all the money out of our joint account and went.

I have never regretted it.

Llangwynnon Remembered

Maiken Bagley

Llangwynnon Remembered

Do you remember Llangwynnon? It stood upon the slopes beyond Bedwas. No-one remembers the little village now. No-one remembers the ancient white church of St. Illian that rose above the dirty huddle of terraces. The church was portrayed on Christmas cards every year but its memory and legacy are gone, along with every structure and living being within the parish. It is eradicated from mind, from history and from this world and only the birds seem to understand. They sit in the green fields where once the village lay. There, they nested in chimney pots and looming trees and now it is all gone. Now they are flotsam of a sunken world, cursed to drift where they left their mates and nests one fateful night. I know it is at the back of your mind. The name is familiar to you and so it should be. You may well have been there, maybe you knew people who lived there, but your mind has barred those thoughts now. No-one else remembers what befell that place for I alone made it out to remember what went wrong in Llangwynnon.

I am Rufus Crane and I have been caretaker of the church of St. Illian in Llangwynnon for nearly ten years. I took over when my father retired due to ill health. There was always, as long as anyone remembers, a member of my family tending the old church. The Crane family has supplied caretakers, gardeners, cleaners as well as bell-ringers, choirboys and organists to St. Illian's through the ages and we have always looked after the place diligently.

My father died a few weeks ago in a haze of morphine. He lay shrunken and devoured by his illness in a crisp hospital bed. His laborious breaths hissed a slow and obscure count down to the end. He whispered strange words upon his precious air. I fancied he was trying to make sense of those garbled images and memories that came to him as consciousness ebbed and flowed with his waning life. I sat by his bed puzzling on the meaning of it all, feeling numb and unemotional.

'Vile Belnes, take me, Vile Belnes, Vile Belnes, Vile Belnes.' He hissed these words whenever his lungs were able to expel enough air.

And I sat by him and stroked his hand and murmured helplessly and patronisingly, 'Yes, Dad, it is a terrible illness, terrible it is.'

But I knew even then he was talking of something else, for the words Vile Belnes had always been favoured by him as a potent curse:

'*Vile Belnes take me*!' he had said when he learned my sister was pregnant at 16.

'*Vile Belnes below*,' he had snarled when he later learned she'd had an abortion. And my mother had glared at him with fury, for there was something about that curse that was worse than any other.

When he lay there dying, possessed by an illness quelling his life, I wondered then if the Vile Belnes did in fact have him.

As a child I once had asked the old priest of St. Illian what Vile Belnes meant. Three boys from the choir had dared me and I, as ever, willingly took on their challenge. The old priest never replied but swung me a completely unexpected and very painful slap. The choir boys howled and laughed at me when I reported back to them. 'What did you expect, man?' they jeered and re-enacted the old priest's swing.

When my father eventually died and fell silent that old curse kept haunting me. Had he in fact spoken those words upon his last breath? The night before his funeral I went and sat in the Church of St. Illian in Llangwynnon. I sat there and stared at the pews my father had mended, the walls that he had painted and the small window panes that he had painstakingly replaced. This place was a legend of my family and yet we Cranes were ever the servants, unseen, unrecognised and unobtrusive. We Cranes would fix and clean and mend and the congregation would barely notice us.

There were wilting flowers in the vases at the ends of the pews that night, left over from a wedding earlier in the day. There was a smell of soil and spoiled water. A few votive candles burned by the side of the altar and I went there to make my contribution, wincing as I walked the aisle, for I found it offensive that people had been married here today, when my father would be buried here tomorrow. I wondered if they would leave the wilting leftovers from the happy celebrations here for him, rotten and dying as they now were. I felt angry with the flowers (how ridiculous!) my eyes were filling with tears of despair. I hated crying, it was so useless, so I cursed like my father.

'Vile Belnes take me,' I whispered bitterly and jumped when I realised that I was not alone. Great Aunt Laurel, who had cleaned in the church since the hills were flat, sat quietly on a pew by the candles. Perhaps she had been praying, or perhaps she had been dozing, but as I loped up the aisle speaking my father's curse, she snorted and started and stood up to face me, her birdlike hunchbacked figure filling me with cold horror.

Old Aunty Laurel Crane; I was never quite sure if she was my aunt, or my great aunt or no relation at all. She kept the church and slowly, so slowly, she moved with her yellow cloth and marigolds from surface to painstaking surface. Old Laurel of the Church, a wind-torn scarecrow staggering around doing work that no one had asked her to do and, frankly, no-one could see being done. I loved her, she was as much a part of my church as the font and the altar and yet I was terrified of her, when she turned her preying gaze upon me.

'*Virrobalnes*!' she said firmly. 'Like your father! Try to get it right, child.' Her voice was thin yet grimly precise. A clutch of rotting flowers hung in her ancient claws dripping putrid water on the floor. Her lipless mouth quivered, perhaps tasting words, preparing to spit them out onto the cold stone floor. Her skin shone a dull shade of ivory in the light of the candles; it looked like transparent ancient parchment and I fancied she was at least three hundred years old. Her gaze had me fixed with intent.

Aunt Laurel Crane had taught me much of the ancient church. As a child I sat enthralled and fearful on the cold stone steps by the font whilst she wiped the windows and pews and wittered on about old times. I believe she enjoyed my attentive adoration; I think I was the only child who came to hear her stories. I much preferred sitting here in the Church; my father fixing window panes and Great Aunt Laurel weaving tales. It seemed a better place than out there on the streets, in the sunlight, with children who knew nothing, and cared nothing, for the old church.

'Virrobalnes!' she said again, staggering towards me and holding out in front of her an unlit candle on a flat yellowed palm, as if I was a horse and she was trying to feed me sugar.

Her presence was terrifying, although she was barely four and a half foot tall and I a grown man. I felt she saw right into my soul and that those scrawny yellowed claws upon her shaking hand could easily tear out my heart. But I was of the Crane family, she was my aunt and she was trying to comfort me; her grim presence was unintentional. So with all my force of will I reached out to her and took the candle from her palm. I lit it and set it in the side altar, mumbling as I did so, hoping she would not ask me what I had said. I never was any good at prayers.

I stood there by the candles for some moments feeling lost. Laurel hung back behind me, but I could feel her wily gaze fixed upon me. When I turned from my meditations I was surprised to see that she was gone and all the vases in the aisle were cleaned and clear. I had not heard her leave, but she had vanished with the wilting flowers. But there on the pew where she had sat was a small book with a black and white photograph of the Church of St. Illian on the front. The title read:

VirroBalnes - Guardian Angel of Kings.

I took it with me.

My Father's funeral was dismal. I sat alone on the front pew and did not dare to turn and look up the aisle, for I knew there would hardly be a soul present to honour old Crane, who gave his life to St. Illian. Father Bartholomew Mellows slurred his way through lessons and sermons, looking bored, distracted and more than a little intoxicated. I sat looking at the coffin. There was a simple wreath upon it from me and a curious clutch of holly and pine, which I assumed was from Aunt Laurel. The coffin was plain and cheap.

It appeared that Father Bartholomew and his family had chosen not to honour my father with any flowers. The Crane family had liked Father Bart. He had always been kind to us although he had an irritating habit of addressing any member of my family as Crane, just Crane. Perhaps he had not the mind to make distinction, but I always felt he could have at least called my mother Mrs. Crane. Now he loomed on the pulpit reading of the Valley of Fear whilst his mind was most likely elsewhere. I could not wait for the whole affair to be over.

I returned to the Church that night. I wanted peace and I wanted to say farewell to my father without all the petty interference from ghoulish outsiders. I sat on the front pew after lighting three candles and mumbling something ending in Amen. I had brought Aunt Laurel's book and started flicking through it there in the candlelight, perhaps hoping to find peace. I certainly did find something.

The book was a spiritual collection with awkward translations of numerous texts, scrolls and legends from all over the world. I found it very difficult to read; the language was technical and archaic, but I picked my way through the book slowly, noting familiar phrases or names that made sense, and I was eventually able to piece together some of the author's conclusions.

It would appear that *Virrobalnes* was some sort of spirit in the Earth or Soil. In some legends there was reference to an underworld kingdom, where those who honoured *Virrobalnes* could live forever (I glanced sideways to the polished crucifix on the wall as I read those words). The Spirit *Virrobalnes* was, according to some references, a most powerful Guardian Angel, capable of gifting his followers great physical presence, strength of spirit and even immortality. A long passage, which the author had translated clumsily from Latin, made reference to an East European Warlord who, infused by the power of *Virrobalnes*, destroyed five hundred men single-handedly. I believe there was a similar tale from the Middle East. A much less violent account by a cleric from India told of the healing powers of *Virrobalnes*, as the Spirit brought a young girl back from the brink of death, when a terrible plague ravaged the city slums. Hundreds of people had died but this one girl was saved due to her mother's devotion and the power of *Virrobalnes*.

I was rapt by these tales. I sat for hours upon the uncomfortable bench. When the candles burned low, I lit new ones, without saying my prayers. I could barely put the book down. I sat in the homely smell of the dying lilies and read of foreign parts and great adventures.

I heard the chime of midnight on the night of my father's funeral and I looked up from the book towards the crucifix expecting to see his ghost. It was always like that in the old tales. If my father was to send a visitation, it would be here in his church of St. Illian. I lowered the book to my lap and tried to think of something profound to say to the effigy on the wall or to the ghost of my father. I expected a sending, a sign. Just as I thought I might know what to say, Father Bart walked in from behind a faded curtain. He supported his considerable corpus on the railing around the altar and made his way cumbersomely towards me. The discreet smell of spoiled water from the vase at the end of the pew was soon overpowered as the priest approached me with his aura of alcoholic fumes. He had ruined the moment. It all felt mundane now. The spiritual master of our community stood there stinking of sherry, blinking his small glazed eyes and smiling warmly at me. I thought this hour might be profound and spiritual, but here was the priest interrupting! I knew he would try to make small talk, pity and patronise as he stood in this - his cathedral- deigning to give audience to me, the servant boy.

He came and sat by my side. I flinched, hoping he would not try to put his arm around my shoulders. But as he was about to speak, his eyes fell upon the book in my lap and I sensed his demeanour change.

'You don't want to go delving into those old tales, Crane,' he said. Failing, as ever, to use any distinction on my name, did he actually know who I was? 'Those tales are for scaring children. Superstition is for simple folk.'

I expect my mood was contrary, I expect my mind was weary. I felt patronised by him. I always felt patronised by him, but had he just suggested I was simple?

'How is it any different from worshipping Him?' I snapped and gestured towards the Crucifix, I dared not speak His name in defiance, despite my rebellious thought. I was a child with a tantrum. Readying myself for the fat priest to belittle my query, I lowered my gaze to the book and braced myself for the sermon.

'*Virrobalnes* was thought to be a demon in the soil in these parts.' He chuckled apologetically and as he sat there among the funeral lilies in the weak candle light he told me what lay beneath the ground in the coal scarred hills of the Valleys. I could not tell whether he himself believed in this. But I think he was determined that I should cease my interest in these legends. He maintained, whilst rolling his eyes theatrically, that Hell itself lay under our feet. That the black coal of the ground was created by the bile of the wicked; filtering through from below. This was the kingdom of *Virrobalnes* that the text referred to.

I was deflated. Why should it all come to Heaven and Hell? My whole life I had served and polished and cleaned and prayed and heaven and hell did not care, not for me, not for my father. The old priest still did not know my name. He just sat here speaking lessons of the Bible.

'This has nothing to do with the Bible,' I blurted. Tears were rising in my eyes. I hated crying. I did not want the priest's pity, so I got up abruptly. I bumped into the end of the pew clumsily and the water and the fading lilies sprayed across the aisle behind me as I marched away, masking my emotions with temper.

'Crane!' called the priest, rising to follow me and offer futile consolation.

I grasped the great iron handles of the oaken doors when an almighty crash rang out in the church and old Father Bart howled suddenly and then fell silent.

Silence!

I turned and looked back down the aisle at a bulbous huddle sprawled before the altar, bathed in yellow flickers from the little candles. It felt to me then as though the ground was shaking, as though an earthquake rumbled deep below and my legs would barely carry me back to the priest.

The large man lay still and prostrate on his back. The back of his head pressed firmly onto the steps of the dais. His arms wide and open as if to embrace heaven above. Beneath the heel of his shiny left shoe was the smeared slimy stem of a lily and a putrid patch of water. He had slipped when he tried to follow me and now he lay there awaiting the grace of his Lord. I was not quite sure if he was dead or alive. He was not raving and crying like my father when he died. Nay, the priest was smiling broadly; his glazed intoxicated eyes stared up, up towards the crucifix, up to the ceiling and beyond. The dais beneath his head was darkening as his blood spread swiftly and I knew if he was not yet dead, it would only be moments.

Would he be canonised? Would they rename this old church after him? I felt my legs shudder weakly. I thought how my father died. It was not at all as silent as this, not at all as easy as this.

'*Virrobalnes* take you, Father. *Virrobalnes* take you, Bartholomew Mellows,' I whispered to the priest through my tears, as I tried to align one loss of life with another.

The priest's glazed eyes ceased to twinkle and his smile seemed more a gritting of the teeth. Those open arms seemed not to be awaiting the embrace of heaven anymore, but rather clasping, grasping for anything to hold them here in this world. I think that was when the old priest died. I think that was when the old earth stirred. When his blood ran into the cracks of the flagstones, something deep below took notice. And the Earth began to rumble.

I ran up the aisle and flung open those great oaken doors, and there I stopped. It was cold out there beyond the shelter of my beloved Church of St. Illian. It was long past midnight and not a creature was moving in the yellow streetlights. I gasped for breath. I stood on the threshold between the dead priest on the altar and the outside world, where hard working men could sicken and fade in hospital beds and despair was all that was left, no passion, no fury, no one to blame or to fight, just despair. So I stopped and did not emerge.

A cold hand lightly grasped my lower arm. Laurel Crane stood by me. She was holding wet lilies in her other hand.

'*Virrobalnes* take them all!' I whispered beneath my breath out in the cold night air, out across the streets of Llangwynnon where barely anyone had remembered old Crane. I looked upon Laurel and turned from the door and the village. I could see the family resemblance to my father and to me. She smiled and led me back in.

I cursed Llangwynnon! I cast it below.

Those dark hills opened and everything was taken to *Virrobalnes* Kingdom. Every soul and every structure, every memory and legacy. Though I learned that night that he demands a greater prize. I awoke in the field of the lost birds, where Llangwynnon had stood. The old book still clutched in my hand.

I still await the favour of *Virrobalnes;* I await the power of Kings and the passion of the Warlords. I shall be infused as the warriors of old, my despair shall be purged. I remember Llangwynnon. Llangwynnon was not enough. One day I will find a sacrifice great enough to raise the guardian spirit of the coal scarred soil and then Crane shall be remembered.

The Perfect Day

Janet Davies

The Perfect Day

'Here, have a drink of water and calm down,' Mark passed me the bottle of water, I drank it thirstily. Breathing deeply I felt my racing heartbeat begin to slow and the knot in the pit of my stomach start to relax. How could a day that had appeared to be idyllic turn into such a nightmare?

I thought back to earlier that morning. We were not rushing to get to work as usual because we had decided to take a day's leave. We had been working very long hours the previous six months and had spent virtually no time together. Our relationship was deteriorating and when we were in each other's company we always seemed to be bickering. After one bad argument we decided to arrange some quality time together and, after consulting the weather forecast and tide times, we agreed to spend a day fishing from our motor boat. We both loved our boat and had spent many happy hours on her. Recently, work schedules and bad weather had prevented us from using her much. We both eagerly anticipated this trip.

The morning dawned full of promise, glorious weather, the sea flat calm, we rowed over to the boat feeling very happy and contented. Once we reached her we loaded our fishing rods and picnic lunch. The engine spluttered into life immediately as Mark turned the key. He expertly cast off and steered between the moored boats and out of the estuary. He looked so handsome with his wonderful smile lighting up his face. At that moment I truly thought I was one of the luckiest women alive.

'You haven't lost your touch,' I said smiling at him.

'It's an in-built skill,' he joked back.

We skimmed over the azure sea, without a care in the world. When we were a few miles out, Mark switched off the engine, we let the boat drift and put down our fishing lines. We didn't wait long, mackerel were soon biting and in no time we landed a dozen good sized fish. Their silver scales sparkled in the sun light. We drifted northwards on the prevailing current.

'We'll go back south and try to catch a few more,' Mark said cheerfully. He turned the engine key. There was no response. Mark primed the fuel, but still nothing. I was not worried, the engine could be temperamental but Mark had never failed to start it before.

I sat back enjoying the scenery, it was certainly spectacular. The sea sparkled, lapping gently against the side of the boat, the high, grey cliffs looked so dramatic, various sea birds were calling forlornly. We could have been the only people left in the world.

'I can't get this damn engine to start, see if you can attract someone's attention to give us a tow in.'

I was brought back to reality by Mark's angry voice. Still unconcerned I scanned the surrounding sea for another boat. At the height of summer and in good weather there were always about ten to twelve small boats fishing in the area. As far as I could see there was nothing; just blue sea, not a single boat in sight. Mark was still busily bending over the engine oblivious of our isolation.

'There are no boats out, Mark,' I said.

'Don't be stupid. I saw Dewi and Stuart coming out behind us,' Mark replied with an edge to his voice.

'Well, I can't see anyone. Why don't you look?'

'That's the trouble with you, I have to do everything myself.'

We were soon into the familiar blame game. I accused him of not having the engine serviced, he said I always blamed him for everything that went wrong and so it went on.

Finally Mark said, 'Get on the CB radio and ask for help.'

I went into the cabin and called on the CB. There was no response. The radio was completely dead.

'Are you sure you're doing it right?' Mark asked angrily.

'If you can do better feel free.'

'Use your mobile to call for help, that's assuming you've remembered to charge the battery.'

Mark refuses to bring his phone when we have a day off. I could feel anger and anxiety building up. Checking my phone I saw that I had no signal, we were all alone drifting helplessly with no way to summon help and we were back to our argumentative ways. It was all too awful.

I started to cry and before I could control it the flood gates opened; I cried not just for today's problems but for all those months we had been growing apart. The loneliness, the bitterness, the arguments.

Mark looked shocked at my distress and came to me. He held me and said tenderly, 'Please don't cry like that, we'll sort it out.'

His kindness made me cry all the more. I clung to him and sobbed.

So now I am gratefully drinking the water Mark

has given me.

Now here we are, our perfect day ruined, stranded on the Irish Sea, but I don't mind because Mark has held me and I know we can work it out. We sit closely together enjoying the glorious weather and relax as the boat drifts on the gentle current. Then unexpectedly we see the glistening fins of a school of dolphins or are they porpoises? One follows and the other leads, but our boat isn't going anywhere so I can't tell.

It doesn't matter, they have decided to keep us company, there are about a dozen in the school including two youngsters. They swim around the boat then dive under the water and rise above without making a splash. Their grey skin glistens in the sunlight, we are completely enthralled. We have seen schools before but never in such close proximity. They gain confidence and work more intricate manoeuvres. We feel truly honoured to be treated to such a breathtaking display.

As if by magic, at a precise moment they all turn and swim away. We are completely dumb struck. There is something surreal about this whole day. Then one of the largest animals turns, leaves the school and returns to the side of the boat. He stops and seems to hover. He raises his front half out of the water and looks me straight in the eye, a big deep all knowing eye that seems to reflect centuries - no millennia - of knowledge. I feel I could drown in its depth. He then dives and swims away for the final time. Mark and I still sit silently. The whole experience is humbling.

Eventually I whisper, 'It was as if he was trying to tell us something.'

'Yes it was certainly inspiring.'

Suddenly the stillness is broken by the CB radio crackling into life, my phone beeps at the same time to inform us we now have a signal and almost simultaneously three small boats appear over the horizon.

'Shall I put a call out on the CB?'

'No, let me try the engine one more time.'

He gets up moves to the front of the boat and immediately he turns the key the engine fires into life.

'What do you think happened, Mark? It was as if we were in a time warp.'

'I don't know, I'm just glad the engine has started.'

'I'm not sorry it all happened, it was worth it to see that wonderful display by the dolphins.'

'The whole experience has shown us the important things in life for which we should be grateful,' Mark whispered as he steered the boat towards shore.

The Sailing Yacht Calypso

Julienne Pettit

The Sailing Yacht Calypso

'I'm going to Giants' Grave today; does anyone want to come with me?' John's son Bobby pricked up his ears because he doesn't miss a thing.

'What a creepy place, Dad. Are real giants there?'

John, his father, laughed and explained that it was a knackers' yard.

'What's a knackers' yard, Dad?'

'Oh, so many questions! It's a slang word for a place where old ships and other sea vessels are broken up because they are of no use any more. Please be quiet now, I need to take measurements for some wooden panels I intend to fix in the two bedrooms.'

'It's time to go but Mum wants to do some shopping so we'll drop her off on the way there. Pick up the dog; she won't be happy if we leave her behind.'

They arrived at the breaker's yard and Bill came out of his office to greet them saying, 'Hello, John, what can I do for you today?' While ruffling the boy's hair and smoothing the dog, he continued, 'I see you've brought your young lad along this time.'

When John explained what he needed, Bill added, 'Follow me, but be careful of loose planks and scrap metal lying around. We're in the process of dismantling a ship.'

As they passed other vessels, Bill pointed up to the monstrous ocean ships and asked Bobby, 'What do you think of those big giants?'

'Oh, they are touching the sky! How can you get up there?'

Damp, musty smells crept up from the rotten wood surrounding the place and looking at Bobby made Bill remember himself as a young lad. He began reliving that time, explaining the different features of each vessel they passed. As they approached the smaller crafts with missing sails John realised that Stubby, the dog, was out of sight, most probably enjoying herself, sniffing, digging and sniffing again. He remarked, 'Where's Stubby? Go and find her.'

Bobby went looking, calling out, 'Stubby. Where are you?' He heard his little friend bark and found her sitting on the newly painted deck of a sailing boat, its sails partly broken. Bobby called, 'Dad, come quickly, see what I've found.'

John and Bill were quite startled to find Stubby stretched out on part of a sail, wagging her tail on seeing them.

'What a lovely yacht,' remarked John, 'and such an unusual name.' Bobby interrupted, 'Can we have it, Dad? Please…please.'

Bill was taken aback by Bobby's delight and enthusiasm but explained that it was being restored and was not for sale. John was puzzled at seeing his friend's sad face and waited for Bill to continue, and with sorrow in his voice and a gulp in his throat, Bill said, 'I will tell you the story.'

'This boat belonged to my mother and father, and when they bought it, my father, being fascinated by Greek Mythology, decided to name it Calypso. He was totally captivated by my lovely mother, always referring to her as his beautiful sea nymph, Calypso, who had captured him. He often told us the story of

Calypso seducing Ulysses and keeping him on her island, Ogygia, for seven years, teasing my mother about what she had done to him. I heard it so many times. Eventually, when I was 5 years old, I too became part of their love for sailing and, with my little dog, would join them. The Calypso became our second home. Most weekends, if we weren't painting the Calypso or repairing her sails, they would teach me so many things about steering and navigation. Other times we would join fellow members, with their boats at the Yacht Club Marina.

'Lots of cruising and pleasant trips were organised, sometimes around the coastline or to other marinas, always accompanied by Trinidadian Calypso music with its syncopating rhythm, which seemed to echo the ever changing roll of the waves.

'Sometimes I stayed with friends that I had made in the club, watching the yachts setting sail and what a pretty sight it was, seeing the vessels leave, proudly sporting such brilliant insignias. Of course, I was so proud to see our flag with a sea nymph brightly painted on it.

'I remember one year vividly, when each yachtsman was invited to paint his boat as pretty and as meaningful as its name. My parents painted theirs depicting the island of Ogygia. Picturesque flowers decorated each side with a bright yellow sun beaming down featuring the two mythical figures of Calypso and Ulysses. Everyone was so inspired and cheered when my parents had first prize.

'It was during the sponsored gala that the surrounding yacht clubs had organised, that we were invited to take part. My parents were so enthusiastic and trimmed up the Calypso as did the other members.

The weather forecast wasn't encouraging but all decided to go ahead. Calmly we started sailing with the westerly wind billowing up the sails. Suddenly the wind got stronger and was joined by an angry north-westerly, which gained momentum. Then the turbulent monstrous waves began to destabilize the yacht, snapping one sail and knocking my mother overboard. My father jumped in to help her but both were sucked into the waves. I screamed out, holding my dog who wanted to jump after my father, then I too, was battered by the backward swing of the broken sail and was knocked to the bottom of the boat.'

'The next thing I remember was someone standing over me as I wakened and shouted for my Mum and Dad. I learned later that other yachts had seen what had happened and between them had managed to get the Calypso back to the marina.'

With tears streaming down his face, Bill said that his parents' bodies were never found and the ocean was their grave. He shuddered, 'Sorry, I cannot continue.'

He got up and beckoned, 'Come with me and choose what panels you need.' Turning to Bobby he said, 'During your school holidays, come and help me finish the Calypso, then I'll take you for a trip on her.'

As they were travelling home, young Bobby looked very sad and his father, noticing this said, 'Cheer up, son.'

The giant ocean liners will be dismantled and forgotten but the disaster of the little yacht Calypso, hiding among them, will be restored and recorded in the 'Yachtsman's Journal'. People will read about this in the future, just as they read about the ancient mythical stories that Homer wrote three thousand years ago.

The Pendant

Gwenda Smith

The Pendant

On my way to the shops this morning, I dropped in to see my sister Liz. I said I'd noticed a sports car outside Susan's when I passed her house and wondered whose it was.

'It's Catherine's,' she said. 'You remember Catherine from Sue's wedding. She was Susan's chief bridesmaid.'

Did I remember Catherine? You bet I did. She made a play for my Rob and every other male guest at the wedding.

After a cup of tea and a natter, I thought I'd pop round to our Susan's to see how her bridesmaid looked, out of the nearly topless, pink meringue that had enticed all that attention last summer. I know I was being nosey but I didn't take a shine to her at the wedding - she thought she was God's gift to all the men there. Anyway, off I went to Susan's and there Cat (an apt nickname I thought) was lolling in the leather chair in the window, looking as glamorous as ever. She was wearing a low cut emerald green top which matched the colour of her eyes, her jeans fitted her like a second skin. No change there then, I thought.

To be fair, she did look good, long brown hair framed a perfectly made-up face, but what caught my eye straight away was the heavy gold pendant hanging between her ample, and over exposed, boobs.

Susan introduced us and I could see Catherine didn't remember me. She said she lived and worked in

London and was visiting Wales overnight for she had a business meeting in Cardiff the following day. She told me she worked for the BBC and that she was working on a documentary. She had arranged to meet someone in Llandaff who could fill her in with some details she needed for her programme.

'I thought it was a great opportunity to catch up with Sue. We haven't met since the wedding,' she added.

'That's a fantastic necklace you have there,' I said. She told me she had bought it in Delhi when she was working there in the spring. 'Actually it was a present from a friend,' she said.

'Man friend I bet,' was my answer.

'As a matter of fact, it was,' she replied. 'I met a great guy in my hotel and we spent all our free time together. When we got back to England it sort of petered out. It's difficult to keep up a relationship when you're hundreds of miles away. I haven't seen much of him since we got back. He phoned and emailed me a few times but eventually took the hint and left me alone. It was just a holiday romance really.'

'What was he doing in Delhi, then,' I asked.

'Funnily enough, he was working for the BBC too, but for radio, not TV. We were staying in the same hotel but were not involved in the same programmes. Most evenings we were stuck in the hotel. He was good to talk to and we were both glad of the company. Of course there were times when we wanted to get away from the rest of the crews, to be on our own, if you get my meaning.'

'You must have spent some time outside the hotel. Where did you find that pendant for instance?'

'We went shopping down in Connaught Square

one day. It's such an exciting place. Packed streets, lots of noise, traffic hooting, holy cows wandering everywhere, small boys selling tourist tat and so on. I saw this in a shop window and fancied it. He insisted he wanted to buy me a present to remember him and our time together.'

'That was nice. What was his name? Could it have been Rob by any chance? Rob whom you met in Sue's wedding, who happened to be in Delhi in the Spring. Rob who works for BBC Radio, my husband, who bought me a lovely present from Delhi. A fantastic pendant, exactly like yours in fact. Was it 'two for the price of one day?' Which of us got the free one?'

The self-satisfied smile left her face. She had the grace to look embarrassed. I couldn't resist the parting shot.

'Who was the one who kept sending emails? Not Rob I promise you. Yes, he told me of the affair as soon as he got home. Told me how you came on to him in the bar one night. Told me that you knew he was married. You bought that pendant yourself when you saw the one he bought me. He didn't buy it for you. Did you possibly think that in three weeks in a strange country, on holiday, you could possibly break up a happy marriage. Think again, Cat! No contest Babe!' … I slammed the door and left.

St. Valentine's Day 1952 - Growing Pains

John Varney

St Valentine's Day 1952 - Growing Pains

The studs of the boys' football boots clattered along the street sounding like the exercise yard of a racing stable. Form 2A is cantering the short distance from Burns Lane Secondary School to the Carrs playing field. Boys at the back of the snaking line shy at the open gates to the girls' netball court, hoping for a glimpse of some filly's bottle-green gym knickers. The class are on their way to the Carrs on a bitterly cold February morning accompanied by Les Worley. He is the History/Games Master better known as Mr. Gig. Before they get to the pitch they have to cross a narrow bridge which spans the River Medan. Mr. Gig stands at the far end of the bridge counting the boys to make sure no one has bolted. There is a very complicated system for the selection of the teams. This involves acquiring a balance between the good players and what Mr. Gig calls the *stiffs*. The boys who have been excused games, either through a heavy cold or a sprained fetlock, forage along the river bank like spent pit ponies.

Part way through the first half, with Boxer Beswick's team leading 2-0, Mr. Gig blows up for no apparent reason, though Tony Naylor has just spat at Brian Fern. Mr. Gig gestures across the water meadows, past the mill dam, past the Cenotaph to the Parish Church. A funeral procession is very slowly making its way up the long steep path to the Church of

St. Peter and St. Paul.

'A bit of respect, boys,' Mr. Gig says. They all stop playing and spitting and stand in complete silence. They are suddenly aware that the Church bell is tolling and the cortege seems to move perfectly in time with the unhurried clapper.

Without warning the need to communicate devours the silence.

'Do you reckon there's a heaven?'

'No it's like Santa Claus; they just say that to make you behave yourself, that's what I think.'

'When our dog died me Mam said it had gone to heaven and would chase rabbits for ever and ever.'

'Amen.'

'Do you reckon the Nazis went to heaven?'

'What about bloody Hitler?'

'He's probably chasing Jews.'

'For ever and ever.'

'Amen.'

'When you die you die, and that's it, I reckon.'

'What's Christmas about then, and all them angels?'

'Well, there you are then.'

A strange fearful silence has descended. Nobody is willing or able to look anybody in the eye.

'When 2A theological college have finished their lecture do you think we can get on with the match. You have a funny way of showing respect by the way.'

Sometimes strange life determining experiences happen as a trivial event, no loud drum roll, no majestic heraldic trumpets. They pass almost unnoticed and unacknowledged ... seemingly of absolutely no consequence; a silent melody that sleeps in our unconscious being. They are mysteriously recalled as if no time has elapsed. Almost a life within a life, inside another, like a Russian Doll. Although these recollections involve so many other people, they are so singular and so intimate.

Form 2A stand on a bitter Thursday morning waiting for their history to unfurl. Thousands of unknown experiences loitering like tiny eggs waiting to be fertilized. All their faults, virtues, hopes, tears and fears snoozing in the soft underbelly of their nature. These experiences will come and go, passing away with no grief, no eulogy. Their journeys lie in some uncertain future unique to each boy. Before they are twenty-five one of them will lose a leg in a horrific mining accident. One of them will play for Notts at Trent Bridge. One of them will try to stab his wife to death with a screw-driver. One of them will move to South Wales, fulfilling his parents' ambition and become a successful teacher.

The shutter of elapsed time clicks and I see the cold grey tubular metal goal posts, leaning at an angle, the purpose of all our endeavours. I recall the heavy brown overcoat worn by Mr. Gig. He had pulled the collar up around his neck giving the appearance that he was staring over the top of some strange fabric vase. The material on the inside of the collar was much coarser and there was a dark greasy line where it had rubbed against his neck. He frequently took off his glasses and pinched the bridge of his nose with his thumb and forefinger. Invariably there were traces of shaving cream like minute drifts of snow in the stubble just below his ears. The smell of Capstan Full Strength dawdled permanently around him like an olfactory halo.

The cortege is now half way up the steep path. The boys become restless reading from their preordained scripts which none of them can change, part of some unknown god's production. They need to be acknowledged and left alone all at the same time, squirming through the narrow passage into adolescence, like a blind potholer. Their bodies, the birthday offering from their parents, frigid, in the cruel winter cold. They stand at the low tide of their lives, so many questions, so many uncertainties lapping at their feet. Ignorant that the whole vista will change and take on a different view when eventually high tide leaves the debris of their lives on the shore of time.

So many things withheld from their faculties, beyond the power of dreams which only time can unwrap. Their portfolios full, yet unopened. The man, the lover, the father jostle for space on the barque that will ferry them from birth to death. Like a snake they gradually shed the skin of innocence and honesty of youth, assuming the sinister coat of deviousness and pretence of adulthood. They have yet to learn that what they seek is a waiting trap, ignoring their mortality, believing it to be a conspiracy spread by some unknown sorcerer.

The whistle blows. The ball ceases its vigil. The cortege has disappeared like a startled mammal into its burrow. Mr. Gig lights up his faithful Capstan, his shoulders rise and fall as he coughs, sounding like an engine refusing to start on a cold morning. They hear the voices of the spent pit ponies, but they can't see them. A man walking his dog allows it to foul the goal mouth. One of the spent pit ponies has fallen in the river...

'I know who pushed him, Sir.'

'Go away, boy, there were enough fifth columnists in the war.' The coughing engine refuses to start again... nothing has changed.

Boxer Beswick's team score one more goal and Tony Naylor continues to spit at Brian Fern. Mr. Gig blows up for a penalty and tells Tony Naylor to get rid of the canine faeces in the goal mouth. Naylor looks totally baffled and turns seeking clarification from his peers.

'Dog shit, boy, dog shit.'

James Davy who was chosen to convert the penalty takes what seems like hours to retie his laces and repositions the ball at least four times…and misses. Mr. Gig starts to laugh but his rasping cough makes a take over bid for his oesophagus and his face turns a strange shade of purple. We watch like Neolithic standing stones fearing to approach him, lacking any star to take our bearings. Suddenly Mr. Gig starts to spit like a snake projecting his venom. He turns and stoops awkwardly restricting one of his nasal passages, he proceeds to relieve himself of the troublesome mucous through the open nostril. There is an absolute silence as if we have witnessed some weird mystical experience. Mr. Gig takes a khaki coloured handkerchief from his pocket and roughly wipes his face.

'I think we'll call it half-time.'

We gather in small groups like patches of thrift on wind-blown sand dunes.

'Did you gerra Valentine card?'

'I had so many they had to be delivered by Pickfords.'

'I bet you had one from Essie Pearson.'

'She does it with married men.'

'Yes, your bloody Dad.'

'I thought old Mr. Gig had had it!'

'If we did that we'd have had the bleeding stick.'

'Tell you what, I thought he were going to heaven.'

'No, God might have let in Hitler but not old Mr. Gig.'

'Do you reckon he gets any Valentine cards?'

'Who? God or Mr. Gig?'

We start to flex ourselves in mock exercise preparing for the second half like young hawks preening their recently acquired flight feathers. Brian Beswick's mother, carrying two shopping bags, walks along the public footpath adjacent to the pitch.

'Brian, cooey,' she calls three times. Beswick pretends he's neither seen nor heard her.

'Is that your mother, Beswick?'

'Yes, Sir.'

Mr. Gig takes off his glasses and pinches the bridge of his nose and says to no one in particular, 'I thought I heard the cock crow.'

'I heard no bleeding crow, did you?'

The second half is halted by a sudden heavy down-pour of sleety rain. It stings our faces like tiny transparent wasps. We huddle together more akin to a rugby scrum than a football match. Mr. Gig removes another Capstan Full Strength, and takes four attempts before lighting it. A puff of smoke rises and hovers above him.

'Big chief he send smoke signal. Me want more matches.'

'You'd think he could afford a bloody lighter wouldn't you?'

'Naylor, that's disgusting. It is you in't it?'

'No it's Brian Fern's breath.'

In the distance the clouds begin to break.

'You've done it again haven't you, you dirty old bugger?'

'My brother says you can light it with a match.'

'It would be easier to light than Mr. Gig's fag.'

'It looks as if it's going to clear up, we'll restart.

Does anybody know the score?' Mr. Gig sounds about as enthusiastic as a butcher boy at a vegetarian convention. No sooner had we started than the icy rain begins to fall once again, even more ferociously.

'Like God said, when he created light, *'I think we'll call it a day.'* Mr. Gig informs us, pinching the bridge of his nose.

'Are we going to carry on, Sir?'

'And some fell on stony ground,' said Mr. Gig barely audible, without turning around.

The spent pit ponies are already standing at the bridge.

We trudge back to school leaving a mucky track of slimy mud discarded from our football boots. It snakes along the pavement like a trail of some huge slug. The class files back into its stables and the spent pit ponies fight with us for a place on the heating pipes. Freezing fingers seem to take precedence over any other part of our anatomy.

Without warning a mass of assorted coloured combs appear. Anything that gives the slightest reflection is sought and there is a sudden outbreak of quiffs settling on our damp sweaty hair.

'Come on you boys, get a move on, you're like a load of nancy boys poncing about with your hair. Get to your class straight away!'

A confused hush falls on the cloakroom, frenzied hands dive bomb the recent creations of our combs. The whole class has been ambushed by a strange feeling of guilt and shyness. We stand for a moment confused and shocked. The future takes on a disturbing feel, our apprenticeship has begun.

'I said get to your class. Are you all deaf?'

The illusion is over, the transportation of all our senses drift and fade. Our life is a palette on which we mix the present and past and the melange is called memories.

Sirene

Gareth Scourfield

Sirene

The back room of the 'Bogie and Picket' was not normally recognised as being a venue for thought providing, ethical discussions but that was not the case this evening. Across the table from me sat an open-mouthed, eye popping, incredulous looking Glyn. The reason he was in this state of semi-shock was that I had just told him that not only had I won myself a woman in a card game, but that she was a mermaid. The effect was instantaneous. Pint held half way to mouth, eyes out on organ stops and mouth open wide enough to accommodate a squadron of flies. Eventually he regained some level of consciousness.

'You're a liar,' he almost shouted, 'and for another thing I'm sure there's a law against winning people.'

'Well that is the point! She's not a full woman is she? Only half of her is, so the law don't count here.' My statement seemed to stop him, but then he was off again.

'Well what's she like then? What does she eat and where's she going to live?'

'I'll tell you what she's like, she's absolutely gorgeous. Her top half is so perfectly formed you could have sworn she was designed by God himself. Her skin is the softest you've ever touched. You'd think she had been painted with the finest of creams. She has long, blonde hair that never ever seems to be out of place. Her teeth are the pearliest of white and her smile; well I'm sure that it could melt the iciest of hearts.

'I'll concede that perhaps her bottom half is maybe not what you'd like to cuddle up to, but strangely enough it was that which first attracted me to her. She was in her tank and it was her smell of salt and seaweed that grabbed me. That smell alone took me back to my boyhood days, of playing on the beach and being surrounded by salt and seaweed.'

As I was speaking I noticed that Glyn was becoming more and more absorbed into my story and although I don't think he believed me, his interest had now been aroused. I continued,

'She eats normal food, although she doesn't always like eating fish as she feels that it could have been a relative of hers. And as to where she is going to live, I bought a second hand hot tub and she loves it in there.'

'All right then clever bloody clogs, what's her vital statistics then?'

'Well, Glyn, she's an absolutely stunning 34/24/£2.80 a kilo.'

'See I knew you were winding me up. I knew you were lying!'

'Glyn mun, yes that last bit was a joke, but the rest of it is true. Honest.'

'Well what are you going to do with her then? Is she going to be able to work? Hey, you are not going to put her in a freak show are you? I don't think that's nice.'

'No, I'm not going to do anything like that and, in fact, I'm going to care for her. She needs to swim for several hours a day so I've started taking her to places like the fish farm just outside the village. I sit there with my rod and she swims around for hours and hours. It's been handy for me because every so often she'll catch a fish for me and put it on to my hook.'

'How many has she caught for you then?'

I looked deep into his eyes and said, 'You are the fourth this week!!'

Snow

Terry Davies

Snow

It arrived in the early hours of the morning, falling as softly and silently as an angel's wing, covering everything with a purifying blanket of white. Then, the clouds parted for a moment exposing the moon rising high in the heavens, clear and bright. Her silver moonbeams bewitched the ice in a nearby stream, causing it to resemble a silver necklace as it wove its way across the fields.

An opportunity not to be missed, I called to my dogs. There was still an hour or so left before dawn so we headed for the forest that adorns the mountainside around my home. Large white flakes filled the air again and as we walked I was aware of familiar shapes now distorted by their covering, absorbing sound adding to the aura of isolation.

Between the flurries I was able to make out the plantations of conifers, ranged as Roman Legions row upon row, staring blindly over the ancient town of Caerphilly they once occupied. Oh, what stories they could tell. The moonlight dipping in and out of the clouds gave life to their white clad canopy, as they swayed silently in the gentle breeze.

Gaining sanctuary under their protective covering we paused for a while listening to the sounds of the night. An owl screeched in the darkness, a warning to all those that scurry around the forest floor. To the unwary, death comes on silent wings.

It was somewhat warmer under the trees; the dogs

appreciated the few degrees of warmth generated from the rotting pine needles that carpeted the floor of the woods. They took the opportunity to lick the snow and ice from their paws. They forever scented the air for danger, as if some primeval force had been resurrected in them; they looked around constantly aware of sounds that only they could hear.

Pressing on we came to the edge of a clearing in Wern Ddu Woods resplendent in its mantle of white. In its centre stood the gaunt skeleton of a gnarled old oak whose naked strength had endured the winters of three or more centuries. The moon reappeared from behind a scudding cloud and cast a probing beam of silver across the clearing. Against the stark background of black and white the oak now resembled Saint Christopher supported by a staff of silver light. What a beautiful world this is! Oh, if it could always be so.

We crossed the clearing slowly for the snow was deep, leaving a scar in the virgin mantle as we passed, stopping at the trunk of the oak to seek sanctuary from the piercing wind. Using him as a shield, we took in the beauty of the landscape. Then Grace winded a fox, a low growl emanated from her throat. A reassuring caress of her head was all that was needed to quieten her. Our eyes searched the clearing and then we saw him.

Sitting at the edge of the clearing, catlike, with only the tip of his brush twitching, was a large dog fox. He sensed our presence, but being upwind he could not pin point us. He sat with the patience of the hunter: eyes, ears and nose probing. Uneasy, and unable to decide, he turned away to retrace his steps, disappearing into the undergrowth. I felt him watch us as we went on our way. We left him to hunt under a cold, crystal moon. He would continue until the cold light of day touched the peaks of the Western mountain tops, but until then, murder walked abroad.

We eventually came to the car park overlooking Rudry Common; it, too, was shrouded in white. Standing there enthralled by the scene, one felt that the world had been healed of its hurt and scars. It embodied a calm, mystical, almost biblical atmosphere, akin to the spirit of Christmas and the promise of a new world to come. Then the birds began to sing, quietly at first, then, as the sun slowly rose in the east, its probing rays lit up the high mountains of the western horizon in silver and gold. Robin and blackbird duelled for supremacy of the mountain as their wonderful song built into a crescendo to welcome the new day.

I Believe

Helen Murphy

I Believe

'Oh God!' Jim groaned as he swung his feet onto the bedroom carpet. His bed seemed so inviting and he was so tired that he would have given anything just to crawl back into it and cover himself with the duvet. But years of discipline meant that as soon as the clock's hands reached 6.30 am, he was awake, though today, possibly, not wide awake.

'What a week it's been!' he thought to himself. 'And you're no use to me!' he silently shouted at his wife who continued to sleep, snuggled down under the covers, the top of her hair barely showing on the pillow.

He struggled into the bathroom and looked in the mirror at the dark circles under his eyes, the lines that were appearing on his brow, the sides of his nose and around his mouth. He had been a good looking man once, but now… 'Oh Christ!' he muttered. Some might say that the lines around his eyes were laughter lines but he knew the truth. Of late, there had been precious little fun and jollification in his life.

As he lathered the soap onto his face and began shaving, he thought again of the events of the week. It had been harrowing. Iain, a delightful lad of seventeen, had been buried. Jim had known for some time that Iain's condition was terminal but he had kept that knowledge to himself. The outpouring of grief at the funeral service had scorched his soul. What do you say when youngsters ask you to explain why someone such as their friend could die when the muggers, drug addicts and ne'er-do-well of society continued to live? He felt he ought to have been able to answer their questions but he could see their contempt at the platitudes he offered them. During the service, they had sung the hymn 'All my hope on God is founded' and he had wanted to scream. Hope? No. He was rapidly losing any hope he once may have had.

He had looked at Iain's parents holding each other up in their devastation and he had been so glad it was they who were going through this pain, and not he and Mary. And yet when he thought of his children, he shuddered. Polly, his little angel, at seventeen, had decided to become a Goth. He had looked on in horror as her lovely blond curls had been dyed jet black; she had then applied white powder to her face, rimmed her eyes in kohl, and slouched around constantly in black. Even her nails were black! 'Say nothing; it's only a fad,' Mary had counselled. And he bowed to her greater knowledge whilst aching for his little girl to come back to him, which wasn't likely to happen as long as she continued to go out with that long haired moron whose pants jingled as he walked owing to the weight of chains and bits of pointed metal adorning them.

Then there was that incident the other week when the police came to report to him that a group of kids were getting drunk and making out behind the graves in the parish church. If that wasn't bad enough, his son Richard was one of them. And they were all under age… for all their activities.

Jim groaned again. Was he such a failure as a father? He worked hard to communicate with the children in school but he couldn't get through to his own. Every time he tried it just seemed to end in a row. No, that wasn't quite true. He couldn't talk at all to

Chrissy because she adopted the lotus position and chanted 'Om' whenever he came near her.

He was also aware of the irritability that arose in him nowadays when he had to deal with pettiness - or what he perceived to be trivial. Mrs. Brown, the cleaner, had gone on and on about the mess in the toilets. 'Just clean them - that's what you're paid to do!' he had wanted to shout at her but, of course, he couldn't do that. He had had to pacify her and smile and smile and smile. And he was sick of smiling.

His ablutions finished, Jim dressed for the day and set off for work. His weariness, his despair and his sense of failure went with him; he had no hope that it would ever get any better … and that scared him. At work, he studied the people who looked to him for leadership and inspiration and he felt so inept, a fraud.

He went through the motions, only partly concentrating on what he was doing and saying. And then, as it sometimes does in life, a miracle happened.

Beams of sunlight flooded through the windows. Prisms of light shone as dust motes danced and twirled. The light grew and grew until it reached Jim where he stood in the pulpit addressing his congregation. As he finished his homily he paused and looked around him. His parishioners were all looking at him with rapt concentration on their faces. He wasn't sure if it was the warmth of acceptance coming from them, or the sunlight streaming through the stained glass windows, but something was bathing him in a golden glow. In an instant, all the fears and disappointments of the past weeks vanished and a deep sense of peace and contentment welled up within him as he led his congregation in their declaration of faith, 'I Believe in God the Father Almighty…'